Skinning Rope

San Francisco Stories from the Sixties

By

Roger Simpson

ISBN: 978-0-9963736-7-8

Copyright 2017 by Roger Simpson

Printed in the U. S. A.

Library of Congress Number: 2017931305

Layout and Design by Pizzirani Consulting

DEDICATION

To the faith and love of my wife and daughter, and in memory of Howard Zinn whose voice and living example kept me afloat with his constant encouragement.

Table of Contents

The Powell Street Cowboys   7

Three pensioners, ages sixty-eight to eighty, live in a cheap hotel in San Francisco's seedy "Tenderloin" district and show us the meaning of friendship and courage. We venture with them through a single day as they attend a funeral at the city morgue and a phony city PR stunt called "Senior Pioneer Day."

In a Country Called the Country of 'Nam   31

A farm couple from Iowa, transplanted to the Haight District, share with us their hate, anger frustration and guilt as they visit the Vietnam Memorial in Washington D.C., long years after their only son's death.

Rope Tricks   42

A day in the life of new cable car gripmen training to drive the ancient cable cars and at the same time revealing the diversity of their opinions and character. "Hammer Joe" Lagano, municipal railroad instructor, instructs them through the fears and joys of a unique job and reveals that he is more than he seems to be.

Attic Wars   72

Is Joseph the victim of his own "blackness" or Anna's white illusion of his blackness? Set against the Watts Riots down in L.A., this middle of the night conversation answers the question.

Mac and Jesus   87

An ex-Marine, retired and just off a six month "bender," comes together with a confused young man in the most unlikely of places, the Life New Way church. Their adventures as newly hired janitors not only makes the church shine but exposes its hypocrisy as well, as it is contrasted with these two men's search for meaning and understanding in a world from which they feel alienated.

Rabbis for Sale or Rent   117

Ted and Breeze, cable car gripman and conductor respectively, relive the trip to Fisherman's Wharf that caused seven clerics, attending a convention, to file a complaint against them.

The Cold War Burial   127

Drafted after graduation from Berkeley, Ted is sent to Korea where he experiences the first dark side of "war" before he is sent to Vietnam and his world falls apart.

Madame E, Parachuting In   148

Ted and Jenny, on the verge of divorce since his return from Vietnam, are invited to Sunday dinner by their landlady who is the cook for one of the wealthiest and most powerful families in the city. That dinner and the tour of the Pacific Heights home of her employer is recalled by Eduardo, Ted and Jenny's friend and neighbor, who is about to vanish into El Salvador to avoid the draft. The tour awakens the "Sunday shadows" in Eduardo's decision and the strange burdens and turns of power and wealth exposed by the house.

Sunlight Comes to Noe Valley   167

Set in a flat in Noe Valley and on the Big Sur coast, this romance, of far more than what is merely physical, brings Ted, now just three months from a final divorce from Jenny, together with Erin who nurtures him through the darkness and horror of combat memories while gaining a better understanding of herself and the two of them.

The First Dialogue   214

Over a period of several days, Jenny and Ted engage in a dialogue that allows them to speak and share with each other in a way far deeper than during their two years of living together and marriage. In essence it is a summary of the Sixties, what it was to them and what it did to them, both the magic and the despair.

About the Author   244

The Powell Street Cowboys

I

It was one of those glorious moments he remembered: dawn's purple haze through the jungle ceiling's leafy green fringe when you gazed slowly back from the sand and the ocean's gently receding tide. There, above the palm leaf roofs of adobe cottages, the purple turned pinkish orange so fast you'd miss it in an unsuspecting blink. *In all his so-called "adventurous travels" that eternal whiner Ulysses seldom gave pause in gratitude to relish such moments* as he and Ruth had so often, walking the morning beach of Quivira.

Mr. Johnson lay flat on his back staring at the ceiling, hands resting across his chest. His head, as if under an unknown power, turned toward the dime store alarm clock on the night table and the thirty-year-old photograph in its burnished stainless steel frame of Ruth grinning proudly next to Bobby at his college graduation. Her face seemed to gather increasing light from the clock's marine green dials whose information Mr. Johnson seldom needed.

His time came from one floor below in the slow beginning whir of the cable car cable beneath the street. It wasn't long before the metallic rumble followed, the day's first cable car approaching the Powell and Market streets turntable. In his ten years' residency at the Powell Arms Hotel, he had come to know time as the quality of light seeping through the tapestry of holes in his brown window shade, as an Indian might

7

sense the cold trail of a wounded buffalo along the barren edge of a canyon. Today, March 10, 1965, the light shown October blue. It would be crisp, breezy yet warm in the Union Square sun once you navigated the cold cast of shadows on the Powell Street buildings between here and there.

Even Ulysses in his own or Kalypso's bed could have known no greater passion, as small and unheroic as his and Ruth's may have been. Patiently they waited in the bleached Mexican darkness for Bobby's child breath to become like the evening tide. *Hah, Ulysses, cow eyed and teary, moaning and mooning about in Kalypso's passionate land, as if he were devoid of a single blessing! God, cleaved as he was to such noble heritage, god and man bound. Yes, his wait was long for Penelope,* but it never ended with her burnt to a cancerous dust on a sheet in the hands of symptom treaters or stripped of house and garden when the bills came due and the pension swindled. Mr. Johnson pushed away the sheet and three brown Army blankets and rose to a sitting position with his feet dangling over a pair of Japanese rubber thong sandals. Money, the illusion we fools need to make a life, and death.

Feeling his pulse, he found it be damnably consistent at 70 beats per minute. "Morning, Ruth. Good weather. Good day, maybe. For what? Don't know. There's the funeral first. Well, ha, dare I say 'funeral'? Went by the room yesterday with Dr. Swensen. They fixed the overhead socket where she hung the rope, and I'll bet that little charmer with brick alley view'll be rented by week's end. Business as usual. Capitalism for all and small 'g', god bless America."

He picked up the plastic shaving gear bag from the night stand's dry warped surface and turned to go. "Oh, forgot. After the funeral, we go through that idiotic Senior Pioneer Day stuff."

Ruth's smile seemed to fade a little. He glanced at Bobby. Kid was always 'mean-going-to-fat,' regardless of how hard they'd tried to drill compassion into him. Mr. Big Shot now. Hustling disposable diapers and toilet paper up and down the New England coast. One Christmas plane ticket in ten years to the split level in the New Jersey woods where Mr. Johnson's thousand plus volume library stood silent and unread along a den wall. What a trip, the mouse wife darting, her antenna nose working, nervous, like he who'd raised Bobby was going to do something wrong with his own grandkids. Some Christmas. A son? *Not like Ulysses' son, to whom no credit for the boy's character was due: raised by Penelope, the servants, the old forester showing him the ways: a boy willing to stand toe to toe in that sun-drenched court yard as the screams of suitors turned to ash before Ulysses' blade and fire.* Ha! A drawn blade gleaming and Bobby would have run, waddled, away like an elephant from a rhino reeking of stale garlic. *And yet what foolishness Homer penned; How could Telemakhos long for a father who was nothing more than a man shape blurred by memory? Blood and spirit?* Maybe in Quivira, as they hiked the beach, he and Bobby shared something? Or, perhaps in spring preparing their vegetable garden behind Ruth's roses?

"Ha!" Mr. Johnson boomed then grimaced, catching himself too late to avoid the scratching, like a finger nail on a black board, that came now graciously muffled by his top coat and two suits from the back wall of the doorless closet. "Okay, Mr. Ward. I'll be over in a minute." He struggled into the brown terry cloth robe with its, in his words, "ballet skirt"; after so many washings the bottom had unraveled into a fringe of varying lengths. *Hardly out of bed and the old fart's after me.* He emerged into the predawn hallway.

9

At Mr. Ward's door, he paused like a diver on the high platform. Without bothering to knock he took a deep breath and turning the knob, let himself fall forward into the dusty gray light's stink of B.O., dry skin and Vick's Vaporub. *The stench of Cyclops's single bleeding eye laid waiting. So many oarsmen eaten; What could Ulysses tell the families? "Your kid got eaten by a giant." The fortunes of war?* But here it was only Mr. Ward's old skull sunk deep into the ratty pillow whose cover he never changed-- "My own smell is comforting, Mr. Johnson" -- with hands over his chest and fingers slowly caressing a full bottle of pills.

"Let me open the window a little, Mr. Ward."

"Better not. Up and down all night with nasal drip."

"Never heard you."

"But I was." One hand releases the bottle to gesture toward the standard hotel dresser.

Mr. Johnson scooped up the pile of nickels, dimes and pennies into his hand like a waiter brushing bread crumbs into a silver tray. "I figure it'll be sun with just a breeze by noon up Union Square way." Drifting gracefully back to the door, he let in some hall light.

"Don't think I can make it today. Sometimes, do you ever feel like going out the way that old Jewess, Mrs. Weinstock, did?"

"None of that now, Mr. Ward. You've got five years to the good on me. You're only seventy-four."

Ward sighed. "Do you think…?"

10

"You know how they are. But I'll try for a couple extra creams and sugars for your coffee with the toast. Come on, cheer up. Senior Pioneer Day."

"And Mrs. Weinstock's funeral."

The word sounded like "urinal" as he closed the door before the voice ended. "You're a kind man, Mr. Johnson" was muffled. *Surely no such men went in the bright ships of Agamemnon and Ulysses to Troy?* He pondered as the hall loomed up before him. Bed springs echoed, and there was a radio in the middle distance between him and a violent coughing far ahead. *I tread between the cliffs with plugged ears the Sirens cannot lure.* He caught himself up inches from the green metal door, big as a meat freezer and marked, "Gentlemen's Lavatory." There was, he thought, something he must recall. What? *Was it about those ships on the dark sea's lap, moving through dawn upon rosy dawn, each morning the crew longing for their homeland?* Just how he'd always felt when they packed, going home after vacation until the following summer, leaving Quivira, feeling as if it was their true home.

The door swung suddenly open and Carter, the mute, lurched past. Quivira, symbol of the mythical Seven Cities of Gold Coronado and others sought in the new land. Had some conquistador paused upon the beach of that innocent fishing village to rest and named it so? Mr. Johnson went in on the outward swing.

"Hey, Mr. J.," Pete bellowed in greeting as he slapped aftershave on two days of blackish-grey stubble.

"Good day to you, sir," Dr. Swensen followed, glancing at his friend, then back to the delicate, precise task of shaving between the top of his white mustache and long aristocratic nose.

Mr. Johnson plopped his bag down next to Dr. Swensen and set to work. His was a round face except for the slight hollows beneath the cheek bones, and his light blue eyes which watched the razor move gingerly around a mole on the left side of his chin. "How's your sermon coming?" His eyes met Dr. Swensen's in the mirror's yellowing surface.

"You pose a most difficult evaluation, sir." Dr. Swensen rubbed the dregs of his aftershave cap on a bony index finger and spread it gratefully across his mustache. "Words for a deceased come more readily in the presence of true friends and real family. Unfortunately, Mrs. Weinstock appears to be without a trace of either." He turned to Pete for reassurance. "Are you absolutely certain that the arrangements will be made, Pete?"

Pete took his enormous gleaming ten-barreled chrome coin changer from the marble shelf above the sinks and strapped it over his massive stomach and against the leather half apron. "Like I told ya, maybe a dozen times, Doc, Mike O'Shannon works at the morgue. It's gonna be okay. He says so."

"It's just so irregular."

"And what a day, Doctor. Funeral and Pioneer celebrations rolled into one. The low rent dining room at the St. Francis where we chow down on hamburger and beans, not to mention reliving our youthful western heritage." Mr. Johnson's eyes flashed between the two of them.

"Mr. Johnson, such cynicism so early in the day."

12

"My tenth Senior Pioneer Day. Your eleventh. What's to be excited? Always the same, year after year."

"Why, sir, through both my ministry and the Bible I have found ways to ferret out the variations in what appears to be the same."

All right, guys," Pete shook his changer for attention. "No philosophy before coffee." His broad, meaty hands gently grasped each man by the neck and turned them toward the door. "It's all the same old crapola."

Moments later, bed made and dressed in his ancient beige suit and vest, the brown wing tips freshly polished, Mr. Johnson stood waiting for Dr. Swensen just beyond the wind in the hotel's marble entry porch. Pete was hustling the morning rush crowd at the corner in front of the bank where the cable car turned around. Pete had enough saved to get them all settled in Quivira. Social Security checks would do the rest. He ventured onto the sidewalk to survey the street with one sweeping glance that ended at the hotel's front window. Inside, the lobby's couches and over-stuffed chairs were empty. Bert, the day manager, was absent from his desk, and there was nothing to catch his eye but the half crooked, fly specked sign in the window's bottom right hand corner: "Permanent Guests, Welcome." He cranked his head back toward the corner. Pete was limping from customer to customer still dealing out newspapers and magazines. He couldn't remember the year of the great waterfront strike, even the decade: thirties, forties? What difference?

Pete was on the longshore then, and Mrs. Johnson worked as a clerk at Hayrand's Wholesale, the giant textile shipping company on the wharf. Weeks passed in picketing and his shame grew; he was at work, Pete was on strike. Theirs was a strange friendship, him bookish and Pete not. It had grown slowly over many coffees and a few beers at the longshoremen's Eagle Café.

Then the police battles began. He could hear the clubs thudding against bone and flesh, the cries, the shouts of indignation, defiance and terror. Then the night came when they couldn't leave the warehouse. No way out. Torches and police, guns going off, longshoremen struggling to protect their own. He'd run from the safety of the warehouse under a black fog moving in to blot out the winter lights above on Telegraph Hill. The air was pierced with the smell of an oil fire down on Dock Seven, and an explosion further away was eaten by the fog. What could just a clerk do? In minutes he was numb, staggering like a drunk, pushed along by the panic in the air.

There was somebody being beaten by the striker's front line over by the tracks. He ran there. Fists and picket signs and feet thumping into the whirling body that kept begging, "It's me, it's me!," unheeded until it lay still, and the longshoremen moved away, calling back over and over, "Scab son of a bitch!" until the body was alone, trying to move in a pool of blood. Mr. Johnson had knelt fearfully. The face was turned away. He didn't know what to do. Then the body rolled over and lay still in a shallow breath. He did everything he could not to scream when he saw Pete's mangled face. He was no scab. He wasn't!

14

II

"Mr. Johnson?" The hand on his arm returned the sounds of the street to him.

When the mistake was discovered, all hospital bills were paid by the union, but Pete couldn't longshore anymore. They'd bought him the paper stand. "Sir?" He turned. "Shall we advance to our usual morning repast?" They walked toward Compton's Cafeteria two doors up the street. "You were in reverie, Mr. Johnson."

"Not a bad state, Doctor." They filed into the cafeteria with others from similar pensioner hotels scattered around the Tenderloin District. The side walls, mirrored from floor to ceiling, reflected their images between the grey metal camp tables as they moved slowly in line toward the service counter. "We should get the hell out of here. Move to Quivira."

"What, sir?" Dr. Swensen asked over the noise of Millie, the old counter girl who never lost her smile and had just banged down prunes and oatmeal for Mr. Johnson, and figs and the same for him.

The question wasn't answered again until they navigated, through pensioners and office clerks who had rushed in for coffee and rolls, to the spot they'd christened their "pew," a couple of metal chairs up front on the far wall next to the mirrors by the front window. "We should get the hell out of here." Mr. Johnson stirred the prunes, not surprised anymore at their lack of juice.

"My good friend, isn't it best not to begin the day with that dream? It's the devil's own scheme." Dr. Swensen sampled the coffee as if it were a fine wine.

Mr. Johnson stared out the window as a cable car rumbled by loaded with office workers going up Powell to be dropped at Pine and Bush for the walk down into the Financial District. "All right, I'll give you this--in ten years of trying I haven't won the Irish Sweepstakes or Publisher's Clearing House. And we're probably too old to rob the bank at the corner. But we could get to Quivira and live off the pension checks."

"But you know that Pete doesn't want to go. Let's put that dream aside. Come on. Join me. Put on your button and prepare for the day." He patted the half dollar size button on the lapel of his blue seersucker suit. Against a white background was a black Stetson hat surrounded by the words, "Senior Pioneer Day, 1965. I'm a Powell Street Cowboy!" Same every year. If you showed it, they'd give you ten percent off until the end of the week at places like Woolworth's across the street.

Mr. Johnson shrugged in disbelief and rubbed his forehead vigorously with his fingertips as if smearing it with lotion. "Ten years ago you never would have said that."

Dr. Swensen's hand wavered slightly as he opened his tarnished silver cigarette case and reached for one of the four Camels he allowed himself each day. He snapped it shut and studied the cover inscription, "To Our Beloved Albert." The slam of it against the formica caused the woman next to him to glance furtively up from her cereal, an old doe by the pond, until her eyes settled on his hand, quivering above the case like an ancient snake ready to strike. The hand withdrew to light the cigarette. "Forgive me, Mr. Johnson. Please, forgive me."

"Just like when Hayrand's Wholesale closed, Doctor: the pension fund embezzled, forty years in the toilet. You see, if Ruth and I had bought the house earlier and hadn't lived so long in fear of another strike, well, it would've been paid for and I'd still be up there with the garden and my books."

"Yes, and me with almost forty years of service to those miserable hypocrites? Dullah, Georgia. I was just out of seminary when I was called to that church."

"I know, you told me. Bucolic, with the emphasis on colic." The little joke was too old now, and Dr. Swensen's thin lips remained impassive beneath the mustache.

"Completely rundown. Nothing but a handful of elderly ladies and a few widowers when I arrived. We had a new church when I retired and nine hundred people at the eleven o'clock service, rain or shine." He glanced with disdain at the silver case. "And this was the bastards' idea of a retirement plan."

To his credit, Ulysses would have never sent a loyal servant to the street. Despite all Ulysses' braggadocio, Telemakhos would receive that gift of caring from mother and father alike when it became his time to rule the great house. "Who knows, maybe Pete has changed his mind since last I asked."

But he hadn't. "I'm a Frisco man, been here all my life, Mr. J." From around the corner of the bank a tall, painfully thin Negro approached, dragging his right foot. His leg was bent outward slightly from the knee down. With eyes blinking wildly, he thrust a dime in the claw shape of his hand at Pete as

17

his mouth opened and closed without even the hint of a sound. "Naw, Charlie, on the house today." The mouth moved rapidly in protest. "No kiddin', go on now." Pete shoved the paper and a couple of magazines under the man's arm and he turned and scraped away. "Sure, them beds sound soft, the weather and food perfect, but you get so used to the wind comin' up Market and up your pant legs, or watchin' these old buildings sweat after the sun warms 'em a little. And what would we do all day? Maybe, maybe if the time comes I gotta stand in line with my piss ant pension check with everybody else, maybe then."

"Oh, you'll come to love the snippy kid tellers shoving back the money without so much as a smile, like you had leprosy. That's a barrel of fun."

They paused to look past the empty turntable at the Woolworth's corner. It was business as usual; Hari Krishnas chanted and bobbed in their saffron robes competing with owl eyed kids prowling for spare change among the tourists; a short, muscular woman with bluish-white skin and a face completely covered with rouge sat at a card table where she talked intermittently with a small teddy bear and then with God on a red plastic telephone. "A zoo, huh?" Pete asked.

Mr. Johnson smiled. "So, you guys are here at ten sharp, right? Everybody that's goin'."

"And you're sure about this?"

"I told ya, Mike, my buddy from the wharf is in charge. No screw ups, I promise. Even if the idea is nuts."

III

Mr. Johnson managed to get them all to the trolley island at ten sharp. Miss Lydia had muscled her two-hundred fifty pounds into the seat next to Dr. Swensen. Pete and Mr. Johnson sat directly behind them with the Olsen twins in identical pink suits and white hats a few rows back. Dr. Swensen sat with his head at nearly a forty-five-degree angle pointed toward the window to discourage Miss Lydia from conversation. She amused herself with one of the latest glamour magazines, all the while humming quietly in her rich operatic voice that usually rang down the hall on any given day as she tended a dozen house plants that either hung from the ceiling of her room or occupied most of the free space on her dresser and floor, some even spilling onto the fire escape on warm days.

Mr. Johnson watched the transition from office buildings to warehouses as the trolley flowed onward. *Are we the sons and daughters who Teiresias, prophet both wise and clever, guides down to the old caves where flesh of bull and lamb lie in the consuming altar flames amidst the chamber's smoke charred stone and earthen walls?*

"Okay, gang, our stop." Pete spoke forcefully but in a whisper, even though the trolley car was empty except for the mourners and the motorman.

The morgue seemed like part of the sidewalk, its grayish surface was sandy to the touch. The grey and black marble lobby was deserted and the elevator out of order. They made their way cautiously down the stairs, Pete supporting the twins, one on each arm. At the bottom, the marble suddenly turned into

19

white tile and a hallway lined with frosted glass doors. At the far end, Mike sat at a marble top desk that was empty except for a small Japanese TV and a clip board. An Army general was talking to a reporter, and he kept pointing at the leveled, smoldering ground in front of them that rose toward the edge of a jungle some distance away.

When they reached his post, Mike lowered the volume and got up with a beaming ruddy smile. He wore a white smock and clean, white canvas sneakers which moved almost soundlessly toward the third frosted door on the left. The temperature dropped instantly as they entered, and Dr. Swensen hitched up the collar of his suit coat as he slowly led the way toward the body which, all but the head, was wrapped in a white sheet and spread on a stainless-steel gurney. Mrs. Weinstock looked precarious, as if she might slide off without warning. Dr. Swensen motioned everyone into a kind of semi-circle and took his place next to her. The Bible seemed magically to fall open at the proper place as his arms rose to hold it. He gazed at each of his new congregation with a somber smile and was about to begin when Miss Lydia stepped forward. With as much grace as her rotundness would allow, and, fishing through the shopping bag she used for a purse, she bought up a bouquet of ferns which she delicately and precisely placed, one fern at a time, around the body, crying as she laid each, tears rolling from her wide dark eyes over the thick mascara and across her broad cheeks to fall against the tile floor like minute drops of decaying blood, until she straightened and backed abruptly into her place in the semi-circle.

"Dearest friends of Mrs…" He paused as one of the twins, with embarrassed apologies, blew her nose. The sound became a blaring echo on the tile walls lined with metal file cabinet coffins. "Friends of Mrs. Ada Weinstock, her untimely demise touches each of us with its sorrow. But great God's way is not the way of remorse." He adjusted the gold rimmed dime store spectacles on the bridge of his nose. "Like the lilies of the field, our Lord will care for her."

"But, dear Doctor...?" Miss Lydia had raised her hand and taken a step forward.

"Miss Lydia, please, this is...."

"I'm sorry, so sorry, but I don't understand. Those lilies in the Bible, they, why they, sort of, after a fashion, had each other, and the good soil and rain and sunlight. Yes, they did. But Mrs. Weinstock...?"

"Miss Lydia, I ask you in the name of this proceeding, let me continue."

"I will look forward, Reverend." She gave a quick smile and a little curtsy.

"Like the lilies, we will all return to our God through his beloved son, Jesus Christ. And although Miss Weinstock was not of a Christian faith, God's forgiving understanding has shined down upon her, illuminating her soul with His Truth as it rises to meet the heavenly hosts and to know the Divine Embrace." He had moved closer to the head as he spoke and looked fondly down at Mrs. Weinstock. "Dear friends, let us pray. Father, we thank you for thy bounty manifest each day in our lives as we prosper and are girded by thy son's teaching. We have been witness to the goodness of thy servant, Ada Weinstock. Though of the Jewish faith, we know that you hold her now, giving her soul rest and peace. Bless all those here in

21

thy name and in the name of thy son, Jesus Christ our Lord. Amen."

It was Miss Lydia's voice in song that broke the silence. Dr. Swensen raised his bowed head and opened his mouth without speaking. No one knew what the Italian words meant, nor from what opera she was singing, but all remained as if still in prayer as her full soprano filled the bright white room like the first winter flow of maple syrup, sweet and clear from a thick tree. The voice seemed to embrace them in that moment when fear is consumed by peace. No one knew how long after she'd finished that they stood there until Mike opened the glass door and cleared his throat twice.

They remained quiet, waiting on the trolley car island across from the morgue until Pete exclaimed, "Hey, next stop, the Senior Pioneer Day festivities and lunch."

IV

All the way back, Mr. Johnson watched the passing city. He'd taken care of Ruth in their own bedroom. Medication never seemed to kill the pain, or even massaging her shoulders and neck until he was too exhausted to go on and fell momentarily into a fitful sleep beside her. Symptom treaters. Bastards. He was first out of the trolley, nearly getting hit hurrying to the curb, and he walked away toward the wharf past the crumby stores on Market Street.

It was almost time when he returned. The hotel lobby was already filled with residents dressed in gingham and denim, talking excitedly about the year's biggest event, the annual

22

Senior Pioneer's Day celebration. Some of the men practiced "quick draw" with their colored plastic guns and holsters, followed by guffawing laughter as winners raised their pistols in triumph. "Powell Street Cowboy" buttons were all in the correct place just above the heart.

Up in his room, Mr. Johnson went through the usual agony of deciding what to wear. The brown wing tips always looked more like boots, while a bleached out pair of bib overalls from his gardening days over a cowboy shirt he'd bought years ago at the Emporium across the street gave him the look, or so he mused, of a character right out of the *Grapes of Wrath*. His only saving grace was the real leather holster and Colt 45 that Pete lent him each year. Pete always refused to go, just like the thing he had about never depositing his pension check the first of each month. Mr. Johnson couldn't afford a real cowboy hat and was damned if he'd wear a plastic dime store model. He took a long breath and opened the door.

"Oh, Mr. Johnson, how lovely. I'm just on my way too." The way she favored her right leg as she walked must have been the gout she'd confided to Dr. Swensen.

"You look beautiful, Miss Lydia." He stood aside to let her enter the iron elevator. Her tomato red gown was fringed with black lace, deeply cut at the neck so that her breasts swelled together but were modestly covered by what looked to be an expensive hand embroidered white Spanish shawl. Perhaps, she had salvaged it from one of the operas. Though she chattered gaily, her voice to him was the wind in the trees beyond the beach. *Was it like that for Ulysses, on his knees, exhausted in the ankle deep surf, breathing hard, staring dumbly up the beach? Returned from a place he should never have gone to raise sword and strike: nothing more than a tool of the gods for*

the sake of one man's honor, a woman. Had the quarter moon's
shadows in the sand reminded him of the bodies of lost
shipmates? Did he, kneeling there safe again in his home land,
encompass the immensity of his loss, a crazy war at the loss of
precious time with his son and wife, the death of a thousand
young men? The iron door creaked open and the lobby noise
flooded them. Mr. Johnson spotted Dr. Swensen near the
entrance just as he was pulling down his bright yellow plastic
cowboy hat to avoid Miss Lydia's seeing him. He darted into
the street.

"Wasn't that Dr. Swensen, there by the door just now?"
Miss Lydia's neck was stretched and she was squinting hard.

"I don't believe so. Knowing him, he's in Union Square
already."

"Well, should you see him before I do, please tell the
dear man that I'd not object to a dance after the banquet.
Sometimes I do believe he tries to avoid me." Mr. Johnson
shook his head vigorously to the negative on that, but he had a
hard time keeping a straight face as he bid her good-bye and
headed toward the entrance.

Up in Union Square, two loud and disjointed country
and western bands competed from opposite corners. To Mr.
Johnson's classical ear they sounded like an elementary school
orchestra, notes exploding in the clear air without rhythm,
without melody, without continuity. Every path was jammed
with senior pioneers coming from the rooming houses and hotels
that stretched across the Tenderloin District, while lunching
office workers irritably tried to find a bench or spot of grass,
sometimes even jostling with, sometimes glaring at the pioneers.

24

Dr. Swensen's fear of encountering Miss Lydia had driven him to the corner most distant from the St. Francis Hotel. He stood now with Mr. Johnson, gazing up at the hotel's row of flags swaying gently in a light breeze. "What utter joy," Mr. Johnson's lips contorted clownishly.

"Now, now, sir. God's grace, remember?"

"Ah."

The bands were feverish as the crowd began to move. Volunteers from the Chamber of Commerce wearing red blazers with blue slacks, white boots and Stetsons mingled to be sure everyone had their button. "Time for the round up, Pioneers," they bellowed joyously. "Circle the wagons for chow! Let's move across the street. Dreams come true at the round up. Prizes for all!"

Suddenly a voice began chanting, "We're goin' to the roundup, we are, we are!" and the crowd took it up, stamping their feet in rhythm to the words as they surged suddenly out of the square and across Powell Street, ignoring the traffic, intent on their chant, "we are, we are!" The chamber volunteers sprang into action, frantically steering pioneers away from the front entrance and down the side street where a series of doors were thrown wide open.

The floor was jammed with camp tables like the ones at Compton's and covered with red paper, yellow paper plates and green plastic utensils and cups. At the far end, the stage had a blue and white banner draped across it with the words, "Welcome, Powell Street Cowboys, our Senior Pioneers!" Beneath was a table to match the others except for the white linen cover and silverware. Somewhere an organ played thirty second versions of western songs, ball park style.

The two friends had struggled into a couple of seats near the doors, refusing to be prodded forward by chamber volunteers. It took a while to get everyone in place, the noise was deafening, and try as he might the dignitary who was calling for quiet from the stage wasn't having much luck until he shouted into the microphone, "Pioneers, may I have your attention, please!" He had to do it half a dozen times until the noise faded like the voices of geese disappearing over a snow silent forest. "Thank you, thank you. Wow, what a lot of happy faces! Well, well, my, it's Senior Pioneer Day again!" The crowd erupted with yodels, cowboy calls and shouts. "All right then, here we are and here we go. It's my pleasure to introduce his honor, the Mayor of San Francisco. Let's hear it for the head cowboy!" The mayor seemed to pop up from under the head table and strode across the stage to the microphone, arms flailing, as they shouted and stamped.

"Hi Ya, pioneers!"

"Hi Ya, mayor!"

He kept waving his arms, and they did the same until his began to drop like sacks of down floating gently to his sides as if he'd just become aware of them. His speech was short. Waiters raced between the tables with platters of hamburgers, bread and huge bowls of beans, while others dodged in and out pouring water and ice tea. His words came to an abrupt end when he realized that everyone was eating. One more wave and he strolled back to his seat.

Less than an hour had passed since they'd opened the doors, and now they'd begun clearing the tables away for the dance. Mr. Johnson looked at the traffic outside. When he looked back, the mayor and his entourage had left. *Not the feasts lasting days in the house of Ulysses.* Not the long slow meals of summer with Ruth and Bobby. He glanced at his watch and got up. Unexpectedly, Miss Lydia appeared like a bright red fruit from a sea of pudding, causing Dr. Swensen to fall against Mr. Johnson as their folding chairs collapsed to the floor. "I didn't mean to frighten you, Doctor, but you know what time it is?"

"Yes I do, Miss Lydia, though, regrettably of course, I'm afraid there'll be time for just one dance."

"Oh, no, Doctor. But why? We dance just once a year" "Dr. Swensen managed to recover himself and brushed down the thin lapels of his jacket. "Well, you see, the afternoon grows shorter and I must have time for Mr. Ward."

Miss Lydia's broad nose crinkled like an accordion at this. "Only a man of your unbounded compassion would spend time reading to such a nasty and dirty little man. The Olsen sisters told me they saw him buying one of those disgusting homo magazines at the newsstand on O'Farrell Street."

"Judge not, dear lady." He supported her elbow and they moved away from Mr. Johnson toward the recorded music.

They were the first couple to dance, hesitantly, unsurely, until her bulk seemed to take on the grace and lightness of Dr. Swensen's ramrod thin frame guiding her as a knight might his lord's dowager sister. Mr. Johnson stood at the edge of the dance floor. With each circle, she smiled coyly at him. God, how blessed he'd been to know Ruth, *and how lucky the so-*

called great warrior had been to return to find Penelope at her loom, rising from prayer as the last suitor's scream fell into the sun silence of the court yard below and his footsteps were on the stone stairs.

"Mr. Johnson, sir?" Dr. Swensen touched his arm. "Come, time for a quick exit." Mr. Johnson blinked, nodding as they dodged the workers taking down tables so fast and carelessly that they looked to be on piece work. Here and there people sat apart from each other, talking with the space where a table had once been between them.

V

Early twilight came more like the dimming of a dusty bulb on Powell Street, and a fairly good breeze from the ferry building was kicking up on Market as they approached the hotel. Pete was working the mid-afternoon crowd. "Does he seem content to you, doctor?"

"Resigned, I think." Dr. Swensen studied Pete for a moment.

"Sometimes I think that after the strike he stopped living, stopped dreaming. Just going through the motions now."

"Or maybe he has never been lucky enough to have a dream, painful as they may be." Dr. Swensen smoothed his mustache with an index finger. "Just having one dream is enough." Mr. Johnson touched his arm, turning him so their eyes met. "You have lived my dream, sir. Your Ruth. As a young pastor, I wrestled with the Devil every Sunday as I'd look out at the girls and saw only rows of bare bosoms. The Devil's work. Lord, I'd tramp and sweat through the woods in winter or scald my feet on the hot pitch of ocean sand in summer: praying, trying desperately to be released from such images. And, eventually, I would be." He removed his lunch cigarette and lit it, shaking his head as the smoke encircled him. "Since then I've dreamed of a Ruth, a deep and abiding passion undisturbed by the frivolities of modern civilization. In short, a spiritual friend and lover."

They turned into the lobby. The couches and chairs were mostly filled now; the television news showed a series of huts that were burning in the early morning light. When they reached their floor, Dr. Swensen paused at Mr. Johnson's door. "Our usual pew for dinner?"

Mr. Johnson looked up the hallway. It was empty, lit by light fixtures that could have held candles fifty years ago. "I've never been there this time of year, but I'm sure a Quivira winter dawn is just as hard to describe as one in summer. Three oarsmen of Ulysses swept ashore by the gods to spend our nights listening to the guitars on the cantina's patio above the sea."

"Let's keep filling out those damnable Reader's Digest forms."

"And an Irish Sweepstakes ticket when we've got a couple of bucks to spare," Mr. Johnson added with a grunt. "Do you think those that want you to subscribe to something throw out all the 'no's?"

"Certainly not a reputable publisher."

"What the hell's that ever meant?" Mr. Johnson opened the door and was about to go inside when he stopped and put his hand on Dr. Swensen's frail shoulder. "To hell with the usual fare, Doctor. Instead of dinner, let's take a cable car up to Polk Street and treat ourselves to hot fudge sundaes at Blum's."

In a Country Called the Country of 'Nam

That deadly humid Iowa summer was filled with unexpected rains coming explosively with hot wind and lightening; one overwhelming flash took out the storage shed adjacent to the barn. It's charred remains lay in the tall grass even after the house was painted and sold.

The barn was Amish built for Bob Nelson's great grandfather in 1880, and now it was, or used to be, Bob's. There were a couple of long hairline cracks in the foundation from which the spring grass spread far away and down to the edge of the woods by the corral. First, there'd been the temperamental pony who'd bitten just about every living soul that came near it, and then, Redwing, the reddish-brown quarter horse, rider-less but still gentle after so many years, who'd seemingly vanished into the green shadows as if asking never to be ridden again. That broad stretch of grass swayed fragile and wispy, with the grace of a child's hair and softer than the green velvet of a coffin, while above the grass and foundation the wood planked siding was, except for the sunny side, mostly intact. Over there, some planks were missing or cracked open by sudden blasts of wind, rain and shrinking heat. The wood, once smooth as a child's hand too young for chores, was pocked and broken like some jungle road where a wrong touch or turn of your hand drove redwood splinters deep, sudden and painful.

Just a little under a year ago, the roof had begun to cripple. Now large slabs of shingle held on precariously or had disappeared in another storm to let the sky stream down across sagging rafters into the emptiness where Bob Nelson crept, like a hunter who thinks his eyes have deceived him. Flooding pools of sunlight, diminished to chill and shadows the further and deeper he went, passing by the dim grayish cement slabs. There, the milking machine and its white arm-like extensions had been ripped away, and either buried or sold; he couldn't remember.

Was it like this? The air wetter than spring fog by the stream? But the sky so clear, magnified in its wet whiteness. No place to hide. Looking down through the canopy of trees they might love or kill you like the white powdered Jap whores he recalled back in WWII. The wet air. The pressing down heat. Smirks from behind the leaves. "Trees fulla!," he shouted, whirling around, head jerking toward the rafters, sensing danger. Nothing but that damned old owl, its oval shape against the sky reminding him of an incoming Howitzer shell. Bob began to rock, heel and toe, eyes transfixed on the bird. "...yella bellied goddamn dwarf bastards," repeating it over and over, rocking with arms up, pushing the still wet air with his fists until, finally, the owl opened one eye to look vaguely down on him before it closed again.

Recovering as quickly, he saw the corn stretching beyond the rear doors so far that for a moment, exhausted and resigned as he was, the world outside looked like just greens meeting blues. He walked toward what no longer was his, but there was no bitterness for that. "Bastard little monkeys, sons a bitches...yellow bellied dwarfs!"

Silence was abrupt as he stopped, his words cut as if severed with a knife. Somewhere he heard his name. Then, again, "Bob?" The voice seemed to come from inside his right ear, soft and cajoling so as not to startle him.

But he didn't turn just then, his head like sandstone, as fleshy eyelids rose slowly and his gaze found a passing car and the park across the street where Black and White and Oriental mothers nursed and cradled babies as they talked, watching husbands and boyfriends in a rough game of touch football. It was so different than when they'd come here some years ago to buy and restore this old Victorian with its second floor apartment for extra income. Now the streets were a little cleaner and less full of hippies smoking dope or something and playing their harmonicas and guitars.

"Bob, are you awake?"

"Sure, I'm fine." Did he really call out he wondered? "Just dropped off."

Linnell was going to press her hand against his shoulder, but set the lemonades on the glass topped white wicker table in front of him. Those once thrilling muscles had gone slack. She settled next to him on the ancient but freshly painted wooden swing they'd brought from home. It was supposed to be installed on the back patio. It was quieter, but the yard was so small back there. They'd been used to seeing miles of fields, the river and the woods. Now there was just the park, or at least what was called the Panhandle of Golden Gate Park: a long, wide section of grass bordered by eucalyptus with one-way streets on either side. They were on the side that came out of the real park and went downtown.

She began to rock slightly next to him and sipped her lemonade. Here in San Francisco, some days that would have passed like seconds back home now seemed to pass like months. They would never have come were it not for their daughter across town. Such a crowded place where no one seemed to know how to help somebody else.

Just a few weeks before, out on Ocean Beach, the body of a Negro drug dealer, so the newspaper said, was found in his car with three bullets in his young head. Yet life went on, didn't skip a beat, as she and Bob had taken their walk by the ocean each morning, passing the fancy foreign car which sat there a week in the parking lot surrounded by orange cones and protected by yellow tape.

Back in Iowa, she never remembered anything like that. And if it had happened, well, life would have just about come to a stop, what with the talk of it wherever you went. Back home the dead got talked of so much more. She could feel herself almost shaking as she sighed. "Have some lemonade."

He picked up the glass and drank a little. "Yes." He turned and looked at her for the first time. "There's another remodel on Haight Street." She nodded. From the day they arrived, he'd kept track of the change in what had been the historical neighborhood of the sixties. He paused to watch the afternoon traffic and mumbled something.

"What?"

"The suitcases."

"I'll bring them down. I want to take some sewing for the plane."

"I'll bring 'em for you."

"Wait for the paper. They aren't heavy."

34

Up in the attic was where he'd begun the remodel, and it went non-stop, their son-in-law pitching in on weekends when he could, hammering and sawing from breakfast to supper, until two years later Bob'd reached the white picket fence, built to keep stray and neighborhood dogs off his "pride and joy" front lawn, as weed-less and smooth as a golf course. Now, he just puttered and did the yard. She stared out of the large oval window where on winter days when rain drummed the roof, the trees across in the park took on the shapes of plains clouds in the mist and fog. When she'd sit by the window and sew, it was kind of like flying; nothing seemed real down below. People mugged. Another stabbing out by the Giants' baseball stadium at Hunters Point. If you let yourself, it all became one numbing, unending fear.

What was the difference really? Every step in the jungle a numbing, unending fear. That's what Michael's letters kept telling her without saying the words. There was nothing.... Linnell stood with a suitcase in each hand and wept softly, her tears falling reluctantly as if in slow motion. "Oh, Bob. Please," she whispered as she went downstairs, only stopping to wipe her eyes when she thought it was him coming up. Though it was just supper time, she wanted to go to bed.

There was only the hint of daylight in the room when he stirred next to her. She'd been awake for an hour. Everything was ready. They ate cold cereal in the pre-dawn silence and checked the doors twice.

On the airport bus, through the fussing with suitcases and tickets, and, finally, on board the plane, they could just as easily have been traveling alone: the few words passing between them like so much steam from a tea pot pressing through your fingers. She needed to talk, yet the whine of the jet engines encouraged silence. Linnell tried to keep her thoughts on the movie, some foolish and violent thing about New York gangsters, but soon her eyes drifted toward Bob who dozed, slumped over, his head resting half on the seat and half on the panel next to the window. It wasn't that she loved him any the less. Yet how could you tell, the years ebbing away like lost dreams? She got up gingerly and walked slowly back to the bathroom.

The compartment was so small and the lights around the mirror so bright that she had to squint until her face and body became clear. Her long, greyish brown hair with its sun-blonde streaks still had some luster. She was grateful for that and her smooth skin. Linnell studied her face and body. Her figure was still good.

He could never speak about her eyes or hair or slim figure. She'd always said the words that made it all right, as if making love to herself, or so it sometimes seemed. That wasn't fair. He was as caring as he knew how to be, and the first five years of marriage were so. Even after Michael and his sister were born, there was for a long time, tenderness.

The rattling of the door latch made her realize she'd been crying. What was it they had done wrong? They'd worked hard. They'd gone to church, saved, and tried to be kind and caring of others. They'd helped people when they could. "What did we do?" she whispered to the mirror, trying desperately to cut off her tears and put on some fresh make up. "What did we do?"

When Linnell returned to her seat, Bob was looking out the window and drinking some coffee. "Home," he said with a half-smile as he nodded toward the endless cross sections of brown and green patchwork earth below.

"Bob?" He turned away slightly as if the tone of his name sounded like someone calling in a dream. "I need to talk a little." He glanced back at her, then back to the window.

"What's there to talk about? Nothing to say, Linnell." His words echoing back vanished into the noisy engines and the sky.

"Michael." She reached over and touched the back of his hand on the arm rest. When it didn't move, she let hers drift down and away into her lap. "We never really talk. All this time. You know the doctor said we should try. A little more, that's all."

His head partially nodded, then stopped. "All right, you're right." He stared at the seat pocket in front of him. "I just don't understand about talk, Linnell. Mike's been gone since May of '68, all these years. We sold the farm and that life is gone. Now we live in a big city with a make-believe sort of park across from us and more noise than it would have taken twenty-five years to make at home, including all the trips to town."

"But don't you see, we never really have talked it out. It's....what is our life now? What does it mean but sometimes days of hurt, thinking about him, of what could have been but wasn't?"

He twisted towards her almost fiercely, but settled back against the purple seat cover. His face seemed to come slowly to life, a series of red hues through the paleness. "I don't want but what can't be. We're doing okay. Doctor also said we just might go on mourning." He brushed her hand.

They sat for a long time in silence until the stewardess came to pick up his plastic cup. Before his head went back to the place between the seat and wall panel, he turned just a hair and looked at her over his shoulder. "Linnell, I'm sorry." Then he laid back.

Bob stayed like that the rest of the flight while she tried to watch the movie, then began to sew, and, finally, muffled her ears with country and western music she turned so low that its sounds were more like her imagination. Settling back, Linnell tried to sleep too, but all the lost images that permeated the darkness kept her eyes open. It was so useless, utterly and completely, to reach out for memories with no hope of a future. They all now seemed like just clichés; summer, fixing breakfast at 5 a.m. before the four of them entered the first light, feeling the wet breath of humidity as they walked, Bob and Michael with the fishing gear, she and Gail with their lunch basket, down to the river and beyond the whinnying of Redwing to hike through the woods the mile and a half over to the pond where they'd fish and swim and lie in the grass, deep, thick and dry along the water's edge. Freezing in the old county grandstand for Friday night high school football games. Michael's first real girlfriend coming home with him for supper. Viewed from the ascending plane, the bright incidents of memory were so pale. The landing gear clunked into place, startling her and waking Bob as they touched down in a white, summer fog.

Until lunch the next day, their group toured the Capital, the monuments and libraries, the buildings of government. There were several hundred from California, but no one they knew. Linnell stuck close to Bob. They were both a little awed by the whole thing as noon approached and her stomach began to tighten just below the ribs like it had all her life before a school play, an examination, even the morning of her marriage.

Looking from the bus window as they made their way across town to their final destination, she was struck by the horrible contrasts of the city. For just a moment Linnell envisioned all the images of Washington D.C. that she's seen on TV: the shootings, the drugs and bombings, beautiful homes, filthy streets and pale, overweight policemen in short sleeved, blue summer shirts, the hearings and Congressional investigations, the falsehoods and presidents giving State of the Union speeches, and, ultimately, this wall coming out of the distance towards her. Instinctually, she grabbed Bob's hand, and, for an instant, he met its pressure with his own as the bus came to a rough stop.

As they filed forward, surrounded by bright, green perfectly tended grass and a smoky sky, she wondered if anybody was like them, asking, "Why, why?'" pleading to know what they had done wrong, what errors and sins they caused or committed that would bring them to this place. It didn't seem to matter much anymore. Then she saw it for the first time.

The Vietnam Memorial. The wall of granite, black like dried blood in the thick air, was sunk between the folds of rolling green mounds, and from a distance it looked like the partially buried blade of a dull sword. Once enveloped by the stone, Linnell felt like there was no way out. She knew that it had been too many years for this pilgrimage to be called a procession of mourners, the world's attention having mostly passed over that now, what with the war ended. No, they were just left, each searching for a letter of the alphabet to start a name, like blind

39

people reaching out, hoping to touch something more than the smooth deeply polished blackness.

Bob was a little ahead of her. Everyone was so different: people like them, Vets in shabby uniforms or wearing beards and berets and motorcycle jackets. Many were people you'd be afraid of somewhere else. She stopped. The tears were slow to come but began as she watched Bob touch the wall.

"Over here, Linnell." His voice wrenched its way across the space between them. "Linnell?"

She whirled around. Can this be all there is? There was no reason to be there. None. God. She crushed against an enormous man, startled as his long, uncombed beard touched her forehead, and she saw the silver ring in his left ear.

"Can I help you, M'am?" He gently touched her arm, supporting her. She tried to smile and turned back.

"Are you gonna be okay, Linnell?" Bob was next to her. She couldn't remember the last time he'd looked her straight in the eye.

"Yes, I am, Bob."

"Come over then." They move deeper, closer to the stone.

She was clutching his arm now, and his hands held onto her, caressing and caressing, as if that would stop the tears that choked away something she was trying to tell him. They were kneeling suddenly, almost losing their balance as he reached out and pointed, touching the name, guiding her hand which fought against it until the last when the smooth stone touched her finger tips. Linnell's fingers groped across the letters, trying desperately to touch the impression beneath the polished surface, while her breath rose and fell like the varying wind in an ocean shell.

Their fingers kept colliding, then the hands would meet and fall away like the senseless, chaotic motions of cells beneath a microscope. Finally, the fingers withdrew. They remained for a long time on their knees, Linnell rocking slowly back and forth in her weeping, Bob as still as the tears at the brink of his eyes, until the sun shifted away, leaving them in the long shadow of black granite.

Rope Tricks

Joe Lagano was called "Hammer Joe" at his job as chief instructor for the San Francisco Municipal Railroad Cable Car Division. Yeah, he was tough, fair and sturdy, but nicknames are sometimes deceiving.

The bad back rested against one of the outside, wooden ribbed benches on a Powell Street cable car. As always, his less than tall, stout frame was dressed in gray slacks and black Wellingtons, white shirt and blue knit tie under a ratty blue sweater and light tan tweed sport coat. The solemn dark brown Derby was in sharp contrast to his ruddy cheeks which, when he got excited, looked like too much vino. One black gloved hand leaning on the top of the bench held his pipe whose rim had become a series of craters after thirty years in use.

He and the cable car were at the "launch pad," his name for it, the exit gate from the yard where the cars merged with the tracks on the steep incline of Washington Street. Joe thought it was corny but called it anyway, "the river of steel and rope": silent, immobile veins of grime and gun metal tracks with its central artery in the darkness beneath the street, the cable of hemp covered by an entwined mass of steel strands. The system that worked without complaint, although not without injury.

The skylights in the cable car barn streamed down fog and misty mid-morning light on the rows of idle cars. Joe's gaze found the wide passage of red linoleum on the far right and stopped at the Gilley Room's double doors which chafed against each other in the breeze blowing from the high, open windows of the crew room inside. Now and then a shout or laughter, the crack of a pool ball, escaped to quickly fade into the barn's vastness. He was waiting for the newly hired gripmen who would soon emerge to begin their month-long training sessions. The new conductors got on-the-job training from an old timer, but Joe never released a gripman for training by seasoned veterans until they'd been with him for a week or longer, depending on their ability and their fear. And he knew fear well. He'd gripped for fifteen years. You could stand up there holding the grip and ringing the bell like an immutable god or a clown, helpful, silent or sarcastic depending on the turn of your mood, flirt with the girls, but you never quite shook the fear of a possible runaway on a slick rainy track, or getting your grip suddenly entangled in a broken cable strand that kept you locked on to it and pushed anything in front of you out of the way at nine miles an hour until somebody turned off the machinery. It happened. Would again. Experience didn't count for much then.

Not a gambler now, but if he were betting, Joe knew that "The Breeze," or just Breeze as Jerome Travis was known, would be a hands down favorite to make the cut. Of course, already being a conductor helped; claimed he wanted to know both ends of the car so he could earn more OT on his days off. Joe knew Breeze could grip. He'd seen him on cold, late nights take over for his gripman once they got over the hill and out of downtown. Illegal as hell. Joe should have called them for it, but sometimes he just had a sense to let things be. Breeze always wanted OT. You could call him anytime and he'd be at work in an hour or less. Yet, rumor was he had two fancy white girls working for him out of the Fairmont Hotel. Didn't seem the type to Joe, but what did he know about types? Even if it was true, Breeze always seemed to need more cash than he had. Joe got up slowly. The pain moved down his back and disappeared when it reached his butt. He climbed over the bench and started adjusting the hand and foot brakes.

He'd no idea how the other three would do. One was a small kid, Benji Washington, who Joe never would have hired but for his enthusiasm and the Tet Offensive from where the boy had just returned. At only one hundred forty-five, the minimum weight for a gripman, he was all nerve ends and muscle. Then there was the big, blonde Pollock from Allentown, PA, bigger than a football player, built like a door with arms that could probably rip the grip right out of the ground, and a face from the flat end of a hammer. Ed Kaminski looked too old for either high school or college. His application showed some sporadic trades work, nothing else. It was the fourth one, a Ted Lawrence, who was the puzzle. He showed up for the interview in a sport coat and tie, a first for Joe. He was a college grad with a medical discharge from Vietnam. But his exam showed him healthy. Maybe a screw loose, but you couldn't very well ask that. Seemed like the dependable type.

Joe checked his overhead signs. They all read, "Out of Service, Training Car." He returned to the seat. His railroad watch showed 9:20. What kind of paper work did the dispatcher, Gonzales, have them filling out? The pipe went into his pocket and he substituted a Camel, his first of the day, and let the smoke just drift out. Take a kind like this Lawrence. Why the cable cars? Why not use the education you got? Joe always wished he could have. He took off his gloves and studied his hands; they were soft and white without a single callous, and the fingers, unlike his body, were pretty long and thin.

The doors of the Gilley Room swung open and a Beatles tune blared at him to announce their coming. Joe tossed the

44

cigarette, put on the gloves and eyed the four figures walking jauntily but self-consciously toward him down the red floor.

Lawrence made some remark to Washington which Joe couldn't hear because of the noise in the yard and Washington's sudden laughter erupted like a sneeze, as if against his will. Breeze led the way, dressed as always in soft Italian leather boots, a black fitted leather vest and skinny, black leather tie. The shirt was uniform blue but the fit was tailored Calypso with its high collar, puffed sleeves and tight triple button cuffs. Like most of the veterans, the crown of his midnight blue hat had been removed so that it lay across the patent leather bill, making it look like a beret. Kaminski brought up the rear, swinging his arms like he was marching, hands as big as a gorilla's flapping in the pale light like strange appendages on the arms of a windmill. The group hesitated where the red floor ran out and the concrete yard began.

Joe grabbed a stanchion and swung down off the running board. "Welcome to the cable cars, gentlemen. Not a bad place to be if you can handle it."

Benji Washington took a step forward off the red floor and blinked in the scattered sunlight like a pup just up from a nap. "I can, Mr. Lagano, I can, man." His embarrassment caught up with his impulse and he stepped back into the group. "Least I think I can."

"Right on, bro," Breeze chimed as Kaminski shot up two fingers in a V sign. Only Lawrence stood quietly with a supportive smile.

"We'll soon see, Mr. Washington."

45

Joe took them downstairs to view the machinery room. They moved cautiously by the twenty foot wheels turning the cables which thunderously slapped the greasy air around them. On the far side, Joe led them down some rotting, oil covered stairs. They entered a low, red bricked underground passage where every flat surface, ceiling to floor, was spattered with tar. To Joe, it was the smell of human flesh crowded together too long and just barely alive.

Leading a platoon in WWII, they'd stumbled onto a small concentration camp at the edge of an eastern forest almost in view of a castle, a German command post and BOQ just taken by the Allies. That was the smell as they flung back the wide doors: soft, dark and mushy to the touch. Most had been dead. Rotting. Ghosts. But not like those ghosts Joe believed filled the tunnels and channels under the city where the cables ran in the moist darkness; these had died standard deaths like conductors who knocked down too many fares, crabby passengers and surly gripmen.

Joe saw Kaminski's hand out of the corner of his eye. It rose slowly toward the hypnotic undulations of the tar covered cable almost head level to their immediate left. "Just like a rope burn, Mr. Kaminski, only a hell of a lot worse." The hand withdrew as slowly as it had risen. Joe motioned them out and they followed, crouching in a line like tunnel rats.

He exited through the corner double doors to Washington and Mason streets. A cable car bound for downtown with some early tourists turned into the curve onto Washington, the gripman gave Breeze a raised fist salute which he returned. Joe held up a short, frayed section of cable he'd carried from inside. "You see, real rope wrapped with steel strands. Your life line," he paused, "and your passengers. Hold

46

on to it and you never go over nine miles an hour. Let go on a hill and the damage could be fatal to yourself and a lot of civilians." Joe pointed at the loose strands. Breeze's eyes were three quarters shut behind his mirror sunglasses and Kaminski's followed a teenage Chinese girl in a parochial school uniform. She disappeared around the corner. "These get hung up in your grip and you jump from zero to nine miles per hour. A jolt for everybody." Lawrence and Washington stared at the cable. "So, Rule #2, you feel a sudden vibration in the grip handle, you shake hell out of it and open the tightness of the dies with the adjustment lever I'll be showing you. Get that strand out, then call the dispatcher pronto so they can shut it down and look for the snag. That is, if there really was one. But don't try to second guess what you picked up. May have been just an abnormal vibration of the cable. Questions?"

"Say, Mr. Lagano, what about Rule #1?" Washington asked.

"We'll get to that soon enough, Mr. Washington." He turned abruptly and walked up Washington to the training car at the gate.

"All right, gentlemen, join me." He motioned to the benches and climbed into the space between them, resting one gloved hand on the track brake. "Mr. Travis, better known around here as 'Breeze,' as in cool, will demonstrate how we launch a cable car." Breeze dropped off the running board and picked up the track switch that freed the front wheels. With the other hand he held the first stanchion and leaned back, putting his body into the motion.

The car was moving. The rear wheels cleared the switch and Breeze dropped it and in one motion was up on the rear

platform setting the rear brake to slow them down in the steep
ascent to the corner. They swung out of the yard with a whiplash
which knocked Kaminski's head against the cabin window
where he'd been leaning with his feet up on the bench. He
bolted up right and rubbed his big head.

"I'll handle the brakes, Breeze. Come on up front for the
view. How's the head, Mr. Kaminski?" Kaminski rubbed his
head again and stared at the street as Joe applied the hand and
foot brakes and they stopped before rolling across the
intersection and down Mason's slow grade. Breeze got off and
opened another switch half way down the block. At Powell, he
walked out and stopped traffic so they could make the left turn
back toward the wharf. "We'll pick up Mason, the easy run to
the wharf. Then we'll circle back like we're doing now and go
out Hyde Street to Aquatic Park. Then, gents, it's downtown.

"This isn't just a matter of pulling and releasing the grip
and brakes, dreaming to the end of the line. You're in a river in
a big, heavy canoe. Hard to stop." They were traveling out
Mason. Lawrence and Washington watched Joe's every move as
if in that alone could be found some secret to ease the anxiety
that grew in them by the block. As the car passed over the
Broadway Tunnel, North Beach came into view through the late,
white, watery light, the sidewalks and streets filling with cars,
trucks and people. Just past Broadway, the downward grade
increased slightly. "Gentlemen, please watch closely." Joe
released the grip a couple of notches and they began to pick up
speed. "I've opened the dies of the grip just enough so that the
cable won't fall out but we no longer have a firm hold either.
See how the speed increases? A lot of gripmen have used this
trick over the years to make time or avoid picking up passengers.
You can really make time doing, say, fifteen instead of nine

miles an hour. Correct?" They nodded. "Now when he wants
to slow it he just pulls back on the grip and he's at nine again.
The problem here is that sometimes that little jerk back on the
cable can cut a steel strand loose. You already know what that
means. This little trick is called 'skinning rope,' and it's strictly
illegal. You do this and get caught, you'll be history around
here, no questions asked. So, Mr. Washington, now you know
what Rule #1 is."

"I got it. Don't worry 'bout me."

Ever since they'd turned onto Mason, Kaminski had
been swinging out from a stanchion to slap the roof or hood of
any parked car he could reach while waving to the young girls
who passed. Most of them laughed or turned away. No matter
their response, he kept waving and smiling like a trick bear on a
gypsy's wagon. "I like what I see," he shouted at Lawrence and
Washington.

"So far you strike out, Mr. K.," Breeze called from the
front platform where he stood just right of Joe's shoulder by the
entrance to the cabin.

Kaminski glanced back. "Bet I get two to every one you
get."

"Two what, brother?" Breeze asked. Washington let go
with another sneeze laugh and even Joe had to smile. Kaminski
looked out across North Beach.

"Kaminski, what'd I just say?" Joe asked.

He jumped from the running board up to the platform in
front of the outside bench. With his arms stretched out between
two stanchions and his head and neck bent to fit below the roof,

his body almost engulfed that side of the car in darkness. "You were thinking about buying a canoe." Everyone but Joe laughed.

"You're going to get hit over the head with one of those canoes if you keep swinging out in space and ogling the young ladies." Kaminski's scalp went beet red under the shoulder length blonde hair, and he crumpled onto the bench as if in some imaginary defeat.

"Mr. Lagano, I'm an artist. Big, huge canvases. Ten by twelve. I get distracted by things and colors."

"Well, Gauguin painted Tahitian girls naked. Maybe you'll add a new dimension," Lawrence paused, "ones in Catholic school uniforms."

Even Kaminski laughed. "Any of you ever seen a fifteen by fifteen honker?"

"Right now," Joe interrupted, "our fascination isn't breasts but how to steer this canoe. Anybody think this river looks the same because it's one long track? Lawrence?"

"Seems so." Washington nodded too.

"Breeze?"

He hadn't moved from his place against the cabin to Joe's right. With his mirror lens sunglasses you couldn't tell whether or not he was asleep standing. But his lips finally moved. "Changin'."

"All the time, gentlemen. All of a sudden comes a big rock that wasn't there before, or a rapids where it used to be calm." The road had flattened. There were a series of gray and beige two story buildings close to each other on both sides of the

50

street, a city housing project. "You folks get the picture: traffic, people, weather conditions?" Joe stopped the car well back from the turntable as the car there pulled away with a near capacity load of late morning tourists.

In passing, the gripman gave Breeze the standard clenched fist, shoulder level 'Black Power' salute and his conductor shouted, "Watch that boy, Mr. Lagano. If he grips like he collects fares, you're in a world a hurt!"

Joe waved, then pulled forward, showing them where and how to let go of the cable completely and glide onto the turntable. After they turned it around and pushed it off the table Joe said, "We'll take five." He lit a Camel. "If anybody's got a question, I'm available."

Kaminski and Washington sat on the curb and lit cigarettes while Breeze, just beyond them, did the same, leaning against one of the trees planted along the sidewalks of the project. They were emaciated specimens, olives with dusty dry leaves. Looked as if they hadn't been watered for a long time, and their appearance matched the foggy, smeared steel framed windows and their stained and drawn, brown shades. The ground between the trees was surprisingly free of weeds, barren, but pieces of paper and candy wrappers lay half lodged in the sandy dirt.

Lawrence studied the track, then looked out toward the ships, shops and restaurants of Fisherman's Wharf. He walked back around the car. Joe was standing by the front entrance. "Where you from, Lawrence?"

"Right here, Mr. Lagano. I grew up out in the avenues."

51

"We got some college guys on the cars. Mostly drop outs for the arts. Writers, musicians, revolutionaries, dreamers and film makers."

"I'm none of those. Just a BA, Business and Political Science."

"You go to State?"

"Berkeley."

"Me too. Before the big war."

Lawrence sat down on the running board. "What'd you study?"

"Music. Violin. Yeah, surprise. I know that sounds implausible. Old man and grandfather played too."

"What happened?"

"War. Marriage. Couple of kids. The usual. Had to find a real job. Not many of those in the music business for violinists. Didn't have the luxury of floating around like some of these Haight-Ashbury punks who can run home to Mom and Pop to start over any time they want." Joe paused to step on his cigarette and check his watch. "Time to head out. So, why the cars?"

They climbed on together and Joe rang the bell. "The pay's good and I like working outside. Maybe I hope there's some romance." Lawrence smiled. "After I got back from Vietnam…law school, going into investments, I don't know."

"I kinda felt like that when I first got home." Joe shook his head as if trying to throw off the subject. "You close to your folks?"

"Closer to my wife's."

"Here, you take it up to the Columbus turn. You've been paying attention."

Kaminski jumped onto the running board and rocked the car with his weight.

"Hang on, men, we're about to get zapped from zero to nine miles an hour."

"Cut the comedy, Kaminski. Okay, Lawrence, it's yours." Joe backed away to give him room as Lawrence tentatively pulled back on the grip, using the release latch on the handle to keep the dies open until he felt the cable's vibration against them and up in the grip handle. The car was moving. He let go the latch and pulled the grip back a few notches. He smoothly reached full speed to a round of applause.

Even though he'd barely exerted himself, there was a light sweat on his neck and forehead by the time they reached the corner and he stopped by releasing the grip on the cable and stepping on the foot brake. "Not bad. You feel tense now, but you'll learn to relax." Joe motioned to Breeze who took over as they turned into heavier traffic on Columbus. Breeze made it look so easy on the return to the barn, back around the block and up to the Mason stop where they came to the first major hill which led over to Hyde Street and on out to Aquatic Park.

Breeze turned and spoke over his shoulder. "You want me to take it up?"

"Don't B.S. a pro, Breeze."

Breeze looked at Joe as he tightened the tension lever with his toe, without bending over. "Not me, Mr. L."

By the time they'd returned to the barn from Aquatic Park everybody had gotten his turn, and Joe took her downtown. Coming back up from the Powell and Market turntable the traffic had increased with the passengers on the cars. Every one they passed was loaded. They went half way up Jackson and stopped in the middle of the hill. Breeze held open the switch and Joe swung the car backwards down and into the yard. It was past noon and Joe walked them to the corner Chinese restaurant. The place was a hangout for neighborhood locals and cable car employees, and they were greeted with wisecracks, shouts and waves.

"You want to tell me how long you've been on the grip?" Joe asked Breeze as they sat down.

"Now where'd you get an idea like that, Mr. L?"

"A couple months ago, my wife and I took some out of state relatives to the wharf after dinner for drinks at the B.V. I'm sipping an Irish whiskey and happen to glance out the window. Who do I see rolling down to the last stop and *then* putting the car over on the turn table?"

"Smooth, right?"

"But not protocol. You guys both know that's a lot of days off." Joe looked at the others. "It's a rule that shouldn't be broken, mainly because of the liability issue. I should have given you both a week off or worse. The whiskey and relatives stopped me. So you got lucky. It won't happen again, for

54

anybody." They ordered the daily special of fried rice with vegetables and a couple of shrimp thrown in, along with a Pepsi, all, in Joe's words, "on the railroad."

When they'd finished, Breeze went off to make some calls and Kaminski tagged along to the men's room. "Be at the front gate at 1:30, gents." Joe ordered coffee and lit his pipe.

"How you keep track of all the levers, Mr. Lagano?" Washington asked, his eyes on the pipe smoke as if Joe was going to blow him the answer.

"The same way you're going to have to figure out how to use your hundred forty-five pounds to negotiate the hills, which is the equivalent of military pressing a hundred and twenty-five pounds every time you pull the grip all the way back. You concentrate and the techniques start to unfold. Then it becomes almost second nature. You follow? But don't mistake second nature for dreaming." Washington smiled as if one of the Big Secrets had just been given to him. "Why'd you apply for the cable cars anyway, Mr. Washington, if you don't mind my asking?"

Washington had a fortune cookie in his mouth and chewed half of it quickly and drank some Pepsi. "After I got home from The Tet, I figured the world'd be different, you understand? Hell, me bein' one of the few Blacks over there that didn't get offed, I sorta dreamed Uncle Sam would be givin' me a special award. Somethin' like 'The Black Boy Who Wouldn't Die.' Kind of like a retirement, like that." Washington barely smiled and looked down the restaurant toward the front window. "So I hung out with the brothers for a few weeks, spending some of the cash I got, goin' to a 'Niner game with good seats, stuff like that, nothin' heavy. 'Course, my Mama had grabbed most of it and yanked me down to the bank to get a savings account. Says I get the savings book when she thinks I can hold onto it. And the hangin' out got old pretty fast. A couple of the brothers I knew re-upped for a second hitch. You understand, steady pay? But not me. No more 'Nams for Benji W." Joe tipped his pipe at Washington like he was toasting him.

"Well, I'm gettin' to be under foot, with four other kids at home. One of those half rainy days when the sun don't even try to shine, Mama comes home from work and I'm watchin' TV with an ash tray full a butts which she hates.

Real nice she says, 'Benji, you better go down early tomorrow and look on that board at city hall where they list all the jobs. City has got to have something for you. You had good grades in high school, and you're a veteran now, no matter if they call it a war or not'. And a medic too."

He paused to eat the other half of his cookie. "I looked and I applied for every job says 'high school diploma or GED, no experience necessary.' This job was my first and best offer so far." His laughter sneezed again and he looked at them.

"They threw me in recon, just across the Cambodian border. Almost eleven months in two shifts," Lawrence volunteered. "We were all niggers." Lawrence nodded and blew out a long stream of smoke from the cigarette at the edge of his lips. "Your Mama kick your butt too?" Washington good naturedly jabbed his shoulder with a left.

"My wife, actually. But she had other employment ideas."

"Well, you been to college?"

56

"Yeah.'

"So you just told her, 'Baby, I'm goin' down to city hall and team up with brother Benji and screw General Motors." This time his laughter built slowly until his thin shoulders were bouncing with it like a hula doll on the cluttered dashboard of an old car.

"And then she said," Lawrence opened his eyes wide and furrowed his brow, "'Who's Benji?'" That nearly knocked Washington out of his chair backwards and Joe had to catch him.

"Careful, son," Joe laughed as he got up and put the money under a salt shaker. "Time to go back to work."

Their car had been taken out by a 1-9 crew and they waited for the mechanics to pull another one up to the gate. Kaminski came running from the men's room.

Breeze glanced at him through his mirrors. "Man, you look like you fell in."

"Me and the people I share the loft in Filmore with went out to the Mission for hot stuff last night. I got a Mexican tooth ache that won't quit. My ass is on fire!"

"Maybe it's not Mexican," Lawrence paused, "maybe it's Polish." Washington bent over and slapped his knees over that while Breeze just smiled, watching Kaminski glare at Lawrence for a minute until he finally got it.

"Nah, Polish food's for the gods."

"Food's over." Joe motioned them aboard and Washington asked to open the switch this time. Joe was surprised at how easily he used his weight to get the car rolling.

The rear gate hadn't been opened, but Washington managed to jump on and hold until they stopped down at the corner.

"That little guy's a real monkey the way he hung on with no place to hang," Kaminski laughed.

"Doesn't look much like a monkey to me, man." Breeze wasn't smiling.

"Ah, you know what I mean, small with those big eyes." Kaminski looked at himself in Breeze's mirrors.

Joe let the car drift across Mason down to mid-block where the track switches were. Lawrence jumped off to open it, but Joe motioned him back on the car, explaining, "That's for going outbound only. We'll go into town. You gentlemen may get a chance to negotiate a few blocks in heavy traffic."

Kaminski swung out with one big arm wrapped around a running board stanchion as the car took the curve and headed up to California and Powell. He knew Breeze's gaze hadn't left him. "Now you looked a little monkeyish right there, but I don't comprende your meaning as to Mr. Washington?" Breeze had pushed away from the cabin next to Joe where he'd been leaning and stood, legs slightly apart, hands to his sides.

"Forget it, you coloreds all stick together." Kaminski looked north toward Oakland.

Joe stopped abruptly at Powell and California. "You two, knock off the crap. We're all about training here and that's it. Got it?" Breeze continued to stare at Kaminski who nodded reluctantly in Joe's direction without looking at him. "Breeze, take her downtown."

Breeze let a slow smile drift across his lips as he turned from Kaminski and put on a pair of well-worn gripman's gloves. "At your service, Mr. L."

They got a green light from Barney Brantingham in the tower where he directed intersection traffic between the big double ended cars on California and those smaller ones coming up and down Powell. Breeze pulled up onto the flat and dropped the cable. The car's momentum carried it to the hill's downtown crest. As they paused, some tourists rushed from the curb, but retreated when Lawrence smiled and pointed at the signs. He and Washington were grinning like five year olds as Breeze picked up the grip handle and caught the cable in its dies with one easy motion. He pulled them to the lip and just over the edge where he finessed the car into the sudden downward arch by applying the brakes, then the grip, then brakes, then grip, until they were over the edge descending to Pine, Bush and last, onto the flat, crossing Sutter in the flow of traffic by Union Square and the St. Francis Hotel and on to the Market Street turntable.

"Very nice, Breeze," Joe commented as they waited for the car filled with passengers to pull away from the turntable.

As they were turning their car around, Kaminski pushed in the rear next to Breeze. "Hey, look, I didn't mean anything. Washington has guts, being his size and all."

Breeze took one hand off the car and lowered his mirrors to look at Kaminski. "That's cool."

"I was raised a red neck, that's just me. I don't like it and it's not part of my art, but it is what it is, just there." They steadied the car and pushed it off the table.

"Mah man, there are Anglos, mostly Irish Catholics, who work here, dig? Just about as many Blacks. You can throw in a few Orientals and a couple of Mexicans and that's the mix. Some of the brothers been turning Moslem since sixty-three. Five years of Black pride growing around here. Now and then the bad vibes get going. Just keep a low profile on it and you'll be good." Breeze extended his hand and they shook, Black Power style. Kaminski went forward to take his turn and Breeze climbed up next to Lawrence on the rear platform.

"How come you're hangin' back here?"

"Thought I'd try to air out a little." Lawrence flapped his arms. "It's too windy to take off this sweater but too sticky to keep it on."

"Righteous sweat, Teddy." Breeze hesitated. "Can I call you that?"

Lawrence shrugged. "Ted, Teddy, whatever, just not Mr. Lawrence." He smiled.

"Don't worry about sweat. It comes with the job, especially when you're new." The car lurched forward and they steadied themselves. "Damn, that Pollock is too strong for our own good."

"I heard what he said up at the barn about Benji."

"No biggie. You'll hear some 'white trash' and 'honkie' talk if you stick around. Nature of the beast, the US of A."

"There's so much to learn. You make it look so easy."

"I've been grippin' unofficially for three years plus another four as a conductor for a total of seven on the cars. I

60

should look smooth. But I could tell right off, Teddy, you're a worrier." Breeze motioned another family of tourists back to the sidewalk at Union Square. "In spite of that, you're gonna be okay. You got the size and smarts, now you just need some confidence. Hell, if Washington can make it, and my money says he will, you're gonna too. There's tricks you'll learn on your own but in no text book. Just try to feel that cable, right down to its rope core. Feel it. Get in the river with it. Joe's not kidding about that. Or the canoe bit." Breeze chuckled for the first time. "That cat actually gets smarter as I get older. He's straight. Won't bullshit you. Come on, let's go up front and watch the big kid sweat."

The car stopped at Sutter and they ran up to the left running board. Washington was on the right and Joe in Breeze's place by the cabin. In just those few level blocks Kaminski was sweating through his wool lined Levi jacket. "Mr. Kaminski, I'll take it to the top." Joe stepped up next to him.

"Come on, Mr. Lagano, give me a shot at the hills. I can do it." He wiped his forehead with the arm of his jacket. It was as wet as his back.

"You better take a breather."

"Just to the top of the hill. I've been watching you adjust the grip tension with the lever. You'll be right next to me, if I screw up."

Joe glanced over at Breeze. "We'll try one hill. But you have to listen to me. You want it tight enough to pull you up there. Maybe a turn and a half, but not so tight you break your back pulling." Kaminski shook his head and took up the turns on the lever. "Right, you got the light. Ease it into the

61

intersection. Good, now pull it back a few notches, good. How's it feel? All right, you're locked on and coming into the upgrade depression. Wait, wait, *now*, all the way back. That's it." Kaminski's face, neck and scalp were the color of watered down tomato soup and the sweat was falling from his forehead into his eyes like rapids into light blue pools as he tried to blink it away. "Get her up on the flat. Wait, wait. Good. Now release the grip, get on the foot brake and secure the track brake. You did it, Mr. Kaminski." Joe patted him on the shoulder. Kaminski hardly acknowledged it. He bent over a little like a man in a full body cast to look out the open front window.

"What are you doing?" Lawrence asked.

Kaminski used his jacket sleeve as a towel again and squinted at them. "I'm looking to see if these next two hills are still there and praying they aren't." He managed the hint of a smile which, given the size of his face, was pretty wide.

Joe touched his arm. "My turn, Mr. Kaminski."

But Kaminski held onto the track brake handle. "Mr. Lagano, let me finish this. Please." Joe threw up his hands and stepped back. "That's a family tradition. We don't do much, but we finish. Let me get to the top and you can throw me off." He released the brakes and pulled back on the grip slowly and the car was moving. Entering the ascent, his hands slipped on the grip handle, even his gloves were drenched, "Watch it, Mr. Kaminski," but he recovered, and with one hand like a man on the end of a tug of war rope, he pulled the grip all the way back and they were going to Pine. Suddenly, Washington was up on the outside bench, bracing himself against the rafter, and started wiping away the sweat from Kaminski's forehead with his handkerchief. The big man didn't even notice, his concentration

62

fully on the hill and the grip handle he now held firmly with both hands.

"Keep your back straight, Kaminski. Swing your butt back and under so your body takes the weight of the pull. Another grip like this last one and you'll make hamburger of your shoulders and lower back fast."

They reached the flat intersection at Pine and he managed to stop. He was breathing like a spent runner. "Son of a bitch. And we make seven or eight round trips every frigging day?"

"Sometimes ten plus on the California line. And the hills are bigger." Breeze looked sharply at Kaminski. "You hear me, man?" There was just the outer edge of concern in his voice. "You okay?"

"Yeah," Kaminski panted. "I was only hoping I didn't hear you. "This last hill's the toughest because there's no signal light up there to stop traffic. You dig? Just the guy in the tower." Breeze cautioned, eyeing Joe.

"Mr. Kaminski?"

"I got it, Mr. Lagano. I got it."

"You're awfully heated up, son."

"I'm stronger than you think. I coulda cracked gooks like dried twigs but my flat feet kept me out. See. There's a couple of your canoes." He tried to smile and raised his right foot a little to show them. "Don't worry, after this hill I'm through for the day."

"I'd hope so. All right, you got a green light from Brantingham. Just remember, at the lip make sure the car is on the flat, as far as possible, before you let go of the cable. Otherwise we could roll backwards, get hung up on the lip and cause a real traffic mess. But you have to be on the flat, remember that. So, release the grip when you feel yourself rolling across the intersection. There's plenty of room, it just looks short. You got it, Mr. Kaminski?"

"Yeah," he grunted. "Son of a bitch." He settled into position, ready to use his weight learning under the grip as he pulled. But as he got the car moving into the depression of the hill he slipped, falling backwards and grabbing the grip handle at the same time which yanked it hard and suddenly into place.

The car bucked forward from zero to nine miles an hour and they slammed into the depression and were upward bound. Joe shouted, "Fusion!" as he tried with the others to regain his balance while Kaminski struggled to his feet, lifting himself on the grip handle. "You're grip's fused to the cable like a weld, too much friction too fast." They were past the middle of the hill by now and the Fairmont and Mark Hopkins hotels were suddenly visible, towering over them.

"Let me in there!" Joe shouted, but Kaminski held the grip handle as if it was fused to his body. "Goddamn it, Kaminski. When you hit the crown and get level, release the grip and shake hell out of it. Remember what I told you earlier? It's the only way we can break the weld between the cable and the grip dies!"

They lurched over the crown like an old steer with a rear end full of buckshot, and Kaminski practically ripped the grip out of the ground, he shook it so hard. At the last possible minute the fusion broke and he plunged the handle forward and wide open. By some miracle they threaded through the traffic and pedestrians and Kaminski stopped it right at the loading zone on the other side of the intersection.

"Take it, will you Breeze?" Kaminski cried as he jumped off, ran over to the curb and grabbed a full bottle of pop from a kid around ten. He downed it in four swallows, smiled, paid the boy and apologized to the family of tourists. They laughed as if they'd fully expected such a thing in San Francisco. He waved to them as he dodged a taxi and landed back on board where the group stood in various poses of catatonia. "Guess that's my best shot today, Mr. Lagano," Kaminski exclaimed through his glistening, clownish redness.

That brought Joe around. "Yes, that's definitely so, Mr. Kaminski. Most definitely." Breeze took over. They headed out to Aquatic Park.

No one spoke as the car carried them through a light afternoon breeze and early gathering shadows. Kaminski lay on the left outside bench in the late sun, curled up like a pile of wet, dirty laundry. With Joe's approval ("Didn't think we had an instructor there for a minute," he remarked aloud to himself, but received no comment). Breeze let Lawrence take it across the ever-changing undulations of Russian Hill until they reached Lombard. Breeze dropped over the hill and down to Chestnut. That was always a stop, but he didn't, and Joe made no objection as if, as he leaned on the cabin, any words of wisdom or action were beyond the point now. Down the long steep stretch to Bay, Alcatraz and the Golden Gate Bridge were consumed in a bronze sun that continued to cover Kaminski's rumpled, unmoving shape.

They had to wait at North Point for the car at Beach to go onto the Aquatic Park turntable where another one awaited its time to leave. It was just past three and more cars were being added to the lines for the early rush hour.

Kaminski sat up as they were leaving North Point. They stopped at Beach next to the Buena Vista Café where the front end of the bar crowd was just assembling. "Mr. Lagano, okay if I go in and drink some water?"

Joe looked at him like a father deciding between praise and punishment. "I imagine that's okay. Easier than getting pop from a kid. Just make sure you leave enough to get the city through the night." Joe watched him bound across the tracks and go inside. He shook his head and sighed, striking a match for his Camel.

"Cat's strong." Breeze remarked.

"I appreciate your gift for understatement, Breeze. Now all we need to do is direct that muscle." Breeze stood by the grip handle, one leg leaning against the right bench. Joe and Washington were on the left one and Lawrence sat on the right. The excitement and reluctant camaraderie of the morning was draining away, and as a group they resembled survivors of some ancient and forgotten combat.

The car at the turntable pulled away and Breeze coasted them over and turned the car around with only Lawrence's help. Then he walked behind the outside of the glassed gazebo and stood alone smoking and looking at the bay. Lawrence went to sit inside and Joe joined him. Washington never moved from his spot on the cable car bench.

"So, what do you think, Lawrence?" Joe plopped down beside him on the circular bench that faced the edge of the wharf and a slanting emerald green lawn that ended in front of the South End Rowing Club building.

"You mean, AK, after Kaminski?"

"No, that stuff happens. I meant in general?"

"There's so much happening and then you add the people."

"They're a curse and a blessing. You know the old saying, 'can't live with 'em and no work without 'em'?"

The first afternoon winds rounding the edge of the glass partition sucked the smoke from Joe's cigarette and he heaved it into a sand filled cigarette disposer where it lay and burned itself out.

"Mr. Lagano?"

"I think after today we can go to just 'Joe' and 'Ted'."

Lawrence smiled. "I'm beat right now, even though Kaminski did all the work. But coming down that hill just now, well, I've got a feeling there'll be some romance here somewhere."

"What about your lady?"

"I don't know right now. She married an achiever. After the time in Vietnam I didn't want to be…still don't know why. I keep saying to myself, 'what's the use'?"

"You're too young for that, Ted."

"Doesn't it bother you about the violin? Ever make you crazy?"

"Yes, there's a numbness I guess'll always be there. Didn't live up to my potential, or what my ego thinks was my potential." He laughed. "Ended up just another working stiff with a tie, who gets to be outside. But I practice every night. Our daughters are both married and their room is my studio. That's a step up from the garage, believe me." He grinned. "I don't know. Maybe it's okay never to be an achiever, but I probably won't ever stop the dreaming."

"I like to dream, except I don't know what about anymore."

"Maybe start with romancing your lady again. Even if a kiss isn't a bank account."

They watched Kaminski dance across the street and down the stairs to the waiting car, his massive arms outstretched like the Polish version of Zorba. Breeze came around the partition. "Look at that, a white boy full a water."

"The barkeep wanted to charge me after the sixth glass."

"You should have started grabbing drinks." Lawrence got hold of Kaminski's outstretched left arm and managed to twirl him once as they all walked back to the cable car.

Joe looked at them. "We'll call it a day a little early. But I'm driving."

Washington was doing some deep knee bends and stretches when they reached the car. "Training for what, Mr. Washington?" Joe asked.

Washington followed him up onto the platform. "I wanna grip this Hyde Street hill, Mr. Lagano."

Joe's hand stroked the air as if brushing that away. The car shifted a little as Breeze boarded the rear platform.

"No joke, sir."

"Don't 'sir' me, Mr. Washington. I don't make that much more than you will if we ever get through this training alive. Benji, haven't we just about had enough quote, excitement, unquote, today?"

Washington didn't move. "I watch good. I learn quick. Give me some trust, Mr. Lagano."

Joe turned and looked back at Breeze through the empty car. Breeze raised one black gloved fist and Joe said, "Be my guest." He motioned to Breeze. "You, get up here. It's your call so you can bail us out if need be."

Washington stepped in, picked up the grip handle, pulled back, and they rolled into the curve and started the climb up Hyde. The traffic light changed for them at Bay, and, with the car still moving, he copied Breeze's motions by releasing the grip enough to tighten the tension, then leaned back, and as the car went into the depression of one of the three toughest hills the railroad could offer, Washington laid his hundred forty-five pounds under the grip handle and they ascended with about as much cheering and shouting as Joe thought he could take in a week.

Returning to the barn, he told them tomorrow they'd start at 7 a.m., and would for the rest of their time with him. They got off and headed for the Gilley Room. Joe sat where he'd sat that morning, on the bench, and watched them go. The gait of Lawrence and Breeze was light, relaxed, but Kaminski was like a sleepwalker, his arms hanging motionless at his sides. Then he noticed Washington's limp. "Mr. Washington, what's the matter with you?" He called after him.

"Nothin', Mr. Lagano. Not that Hyde Street hill. Just tweaked my back a little pullin' us out after lunch, I guess."

"Have Breeze show you how to make out a medical report and stop over to County General before going home. They'll look you over and let you know. It's most likely just a muscle strain, but I don't want you out here unhealthy. Is that clear?" Washington stopped and looked at him. "Your job'll be here if you need time off, which I doubt you will. I've seen just about all the injuries."

The Gilley Room was empty and the light came harsh from the bank of overhead neon bulbs as they put away gloves and hats in their new lockers. "Hey, Kaminski, you're gonna take that coat home and wash it tonight, right?" Kaminski sheepishly withdrew his jacket from the locker slowly, nodded at Breeze and slung it over his shoulder. "And wash the rest of you too." Kaminski halfheartedly gave him the finger, but Breeze just smiled. "Benji, get that medical paper from the night dispatcher and we'll work it. I'm due out for a night run on OT in forty-five minutes. Got to feed the kids or I'd drive you over to the hospital."

"I'll take him," Lawrence said. "I'll just call my wife. You have children?"

Breeze nodded. "Two in Cincinnati. Always got the dentist and private school tuition."

"A motorcycle's no good for a strained back." Kaminski walked over. "I got a car, Benji. Old Army Jeep truck actually. I'll give you a ride in style."

"Man, that sure makes me feel good, 'cause I thought for a minute you was gonna try and help me write up and spell out the words for this medical report." Washington threw a playful right hook near Kaminski's chin and the big man fell against Lawrence as the two of them stumbled back toward one of the tables, fell on it and lay motionless, until their bodies began shaking with laughter.

Attic Wars

     4 a.m. Through the floor length windows open to the morning, a quarter moon's peaceful light crept over and around him as he slept under a navy blue, summer quilt on the white futon. The moon passed his face, returning it to shadow. Light touched the polished oak floor and vaguely illuminated the room which fell instantly into darkness in the moon's rotation above the windows. Such a room was particularly receptive to the changing light, because it was monastically empty.

     No pictures hung on the walls which were the color of village houses in an Aegean summer, a flat white harshness, but warm to the touch. On the east wall where he slept was another set of high double windows that were elevated from the sidewalk. Beneath these stood a low table he'd made from abandoned oak pieces in the apartment building's basement. The only object on its surface was a small desk lamp, also made of wood. Here, Ted studied, sitting cross legged on a pillow with his books neatly stacked against the wall next to a small Chinese lacquer box of pens and pencils. Another white futon with large navy blue pillows was on the north wall where there was an archway to his closet, bathroom and front door. The west wall had a long, low, three shelved book case filled with books but whose top held only a vase of dry flowers and an incense burner. There was another archway in that wall leading to a large kitchen with stove, refrigerator and a wood plank table with eight newly refinished chairs set next to an alcove of windows looking towards the city. There was nothing to the south, and that wall looked like a space so empty you could walk through it and never return.

When the knock came, it was timid, dull, muffled. Then once more. "It's Anna, Ted. Please."

Ted slept on through the wars with his student deferment in the old three flat building on 24th Street off Castro below Mt. Davidson. Two rooms. Sixty a month including utilities. It took twenty-eight minutes flat to ride his BMW to junior year classes over at Berkeley, and seven down to the docks where he worked sorting mail part time at the Rincon Annex post office transfer station.

He slept through the Asian war gathering real momentum now in the summer of '65, and through the one to the south in Watts, South Central Los Angeles, half a coastline away, where the desert's quarter moonlight receded in the resonance of flames, flaring a brilliance of orange-yellow patterns against the shallow sky, like spotlights from the Golden Age of Hollywood premieres. Where the Yuccas once grew, now storefronts were burning through police sirens, a brigade of ambulances, and the pops of yet surprising gunfire after two days and nights into this approaching dawn.

"Ted." Her voice sounded the way a mother calls a child who has vanished from sight. He rose, put on his shorts and went to the door.

"Are you all right?"

Her pale red hair, streaked with grey and pulled tight into a thick waist length braid, was flat and without its usual luster under the entry hall chandelier downstairs. The cigarette in her bony fingers was out. She stared at it in resignation. "One of your fellow postal workers is up in the loft with Joseph. Ronnie Le Croix." The fingers of her free hand pressed against her face as if trying to smooth the gauntness of her high cheek bones and temples. "I'm sorry. It's awful. Could you come up for a few minutes. Short of 'go to hell' I never know what to say anymore when he visits." The fingers drifted gently down across the first wrinkles of her white neck and fell softly into the torn pocket of her yellow bathrobe. Blood red painted toenails peeked from under it like the eye impressions in rocks on the beach. "I've got to get *some* sleep. There's a faculty meeting at State. Nine o'clock. First of the semester and I can't miss it. God. Please, be a love."

"The 'white woman stuff'?"

"It always comes to that eventually with Ronnie and his crowd."

"Anna." He paused, no longer able to find the right words. He'd given up trying. "Why do you put yourself through this all the time?"

"For Joseph, of course, you know that."

"That's not an answer."

"Look, I'm sorry I woke you."

"It's okay, don't get upset. I ask because I'm thinking about you too. Where are your rights, your feelings in all of this?

"I've had many advantages that Joseph hasn't. I can handle it better than he."

"Never mind. Hang on a minute."

74

Ted went in and put on some Levis and a dark green turtle neck sweater. "Isn't Joseph saying anything?" he asked, emerging from the darkness again. "Or better yet, why doesn't he ever say anything?"

"What's there to say? A Black brother in arms." There was almost laughter at the end of her sigh, the way someone might after a terrible defeat. "You know Ronnie. Mr. Hyper Black Militant." Anna tried to take a drag off the dead cigarette. "Joseph and me, in our situation. Who wouldn't be frightened? Who will be on our side? We're the rare black and white caught in the midst of very significant historical circumstances, after all."

As she turned to her own across the hall the outline of her body was clear beneath the gown. At forty, it was still a dancer's. For fifteen years she had danced in several of New York's acclaimed modern dance companies. But now she taught.

"Did Madame E give you a date when you have to vacate?"

"This, and that too. Things seem to always come in crowds. Yes, we have to leave by year's end. So, we have four months, the old dear, though why she wants to lose the rental income just to store her junk from France I'll never know. She could continue to pay for storage and still make a profit on this place."

The flat's door was open and led into a tiny hall. There was a small kitchen straight ahead, and on the right, two archways, the first going to a living room that faced the street with a once wood burning fireplace now devoid of a screen or grate, its interior covered with hundreds of cigarette butts. The second arch led upstairs to the loft.

"I don't know what I can do, Anna."

She rested her head against the door frame to the living room and closed her eyes. Her head moved almost imperceptibly from side to side as if answering a question to the negative. "I don't want him not to have friends like Ronnie. Well, I do, but I don't. This whole Black identity thing has only commenced and Joseph, I guess, wants to be a part of it. He's so much more than a mail sorter for some stupid post office. He's begun to write. Poetry. It would be so wonderful to discover something there. Like a novice dancer, awkward and raw, don't tell him that, but there's got to be more. A sensitivity I can't quite grasp yet." There were two or three open packs of Lucky Strikes and some wooden matches scattered on the kitchen sink, and she reached in and grabbed a cigarette and lit it.

"But I'm the enemy up there too." She picked up a half empty jelly jar of red wine but Ted raised his hand in refusal.

"Just go up for a little while. Joseph's white friend from work. Just listen. Talk. Be there for him. For me. I can't. My 'old white woman' insult threshold gets smaller every time I'm around those people." Anna lit another cigarette off the one she was smoking and tossed the other across the living room. Sparks flew but it reached the fireplace and smoldered out with the smell of wet tar. 'You can have the compassion of St. Francis, and it means nothing to them. You're always written off as a phony. Whitey." She hit the door frame with her fist. "Bleeding hearts. Hell, Blacks like Ronnie don't want to tell the difference."

"But Joseph doesn't seem unhappy. He's great at work. Maybe drinks a little too much, but other than that…."

"He needs support," she interrupted.

Ted didn't look at the mixture of anger and frustration on her face. "Okay." He climbed.

Joseph's cigarette smoke and the heat from the loft's illegal oil burning stove were thick, like floating up into a subterranean density where the air was an effort to pass through. It was 60 degrees here and 85 in South Central Los Angeles. In the rear to his right was a windowless alcove with, like the rest of the loft, a low ceiling whose exposed rafters, insulation and wires reminded Ted of the ribs of a decomposing animal. In there, a double bed mattress without a frame lay on the rough-hewed wood floor with sheets, blankets and pillows askew, as if thrown there at random. There was nothing else except an overflowing orange, plastic ash tray, its rim and indented cigarette holders as black as a full smile of decaying teeth.

Ted looked to the other end of the loft. White cigarette smoke swirled around them as if the air had become a dense series of white arteries and veins that kept intertwining and unraveling as they collided with Ronnie, Joseph and the furniture. There was only a thin space of darkness between them and him. The exposed rafters descended to the floor about fifteen feet away on either side, and in that area he could just make out a rusted bike, a torn leather weight bench and a rusting barbell set, haphazard piles of books, photo albums and storage boxes, whose contents of clothes, dolls, blankets and linen overflowed or partially fell to the rough, dirty floor like the junk yard of a life already lived or forgotten.

Ted nearly brushed against the stove, forgetting it was there. They were sitting on a couch full of gullies that had a stain ridden madras bedspread thrown over it.

Joseph squinted, trying to see beyond the hazy circle of light from the floor lamp by the couch. "Aw rye, Ted, mah man. What you up to no good this early?"

"I couldn't sleep. My last summer school exam today." He shook hands with Joseph. Ronnie gave him a quick nod like he was irritated by the interruption.

A burl table stood between the couch and a pillow-less rocker just outside the light whose arms were pockmarked from sweat and body heat and stained dark where the finish had dried up to expose the cherry wood. Ted sat in the rocker, pushing it back further beyond the light. There were some jelly jars on the table that needed washing; Joseph was using one as an ash tray. Ted had helped him construct the table when Joseph thought he wanted to be a sculptor or build handmade furniture at Anna's urging.

Joseph picked up the half empty gallon of red wine that squatted near his feet, but it seemed too heavy for him to extend to Ted. "Vino?" Ted shook his head and looked out the loft's one window. It faced the street below. The dawn above the roofs was beginning to turn into barely discernible shades of pink. Joseph nearly dropped the jug. The wine splashed around inside.

"What I'm telling you, Joseph, is that the white man's day is gone. The wounds are open. Watts, all of South Central is burning. The rest could burn too." Joseph's eyes were only slits, as if tired or trying to block any field of vision.

78

"I'm hip, Ronnie." Joseph belched and drank more wine from one of the jars on the table.

Anna had come up and quietly settled yoga style on the floor at the other end of the dimness by the stairwell. She'd unbraided her hair which now fell thickly around her shoulders. Her head tilted slightly. Her features were distinguishable in the momentary orange light of the cigarette when she inhaled.

"Study your history back to antiquity, Joseph. Athens, the Peloponnesian Wars. So what's there? Suppression and uprising." Ronnie watched Joseph try to set his glass down evenly on the burl table.

"This isn't a war in that sense, you know." Anna's voice was steady but weak across the empty space, the report of a distant rifle shot long after the trigger had been pulled.

"Not a war. What are you talking about?" Ronnie peered down the loft looking for more than the voice.

"It isn't even a revolution. Not about politics. It's a riot." The steadiness was dissolving. 'This wasn't planned after all, was it?"

Ronnie's right arm and hand thrust that way out beyond the circle of light as if he was trying to push her away with the smoke and heat. "You're White, you need to feel comfortable. What I say is, who cares what it's called, or what its origins were? Down there the town is burning. It could be here too." He shook his head toward her, then refocused on Joseph. "Joseph, I love you, Brother, but where's your pride? Black pride, man. What's wrong with our women? Brother, you know that "flax" is a sickness."

Joseph's broad skull with its thick Afro swayed slowly first to one side, then the other, and stopped. "Nothin' wrong with 'em, Ronnie. Black women. Nothin' wrong." Cigarette smoke crept from his nose as he took another drink from a jar.

"Then why have you gone flax? Picked up this white woman at the Jazz Workshop. And an old one at that. Looks over forty to me. What's left after menopause, man?"

Ted glanced at Anna. She was gone.

Joseph's laugh was like a new cough; it was short, and stopped abruptly. He stared at his hands. "She digs jazz too, Ronnie."

Ted rose and went to the window. Mr. Dobjanski, the trolley motorman who lived across the street, had just pulled his car out and, by its headlights, was closing the double wooden garage doors. Ted turned back. "Don't you think there's anything redeeming about Whites?" Ronnie and Joseph looked up at Ted as if he'd just come in. "Let's start, say, with Jesus."

Ronnie chuckled. "There's the exploitation mentality we talked about earlier, Joseph. See how they taught him? Jumps right out at you." Joseph's head was against the couch and he blinked. "Jesus wasn't fair, he was dark. Probably an Arab. Did your Christians ever tell you where he was from about seventeen until around thirty, just before he really started teaching? He wasn't with any Christians, that's a fact."

"Fine, let's say Jesus was an Arab. What difference does it make? I was talking about compassion. I know people like me and Anna will never appreciate what it's like being Black, but we have *some* feelings. Everybody suffers." Ronnie looked at Joseph and sighed, rubbing both sides of his shaved

80

head vigorously. "Other than Elijah Mohammed, I can't think of any Black leader today who says all Whites are bad. Some of us have the right to care. You can't take that."

"You don't get it, man. This is all about Blackness, embracing ourselves for the first time. Killing Uncle Tom and Aunt Dinah. Looking at what we want, not what some honkie thinks we want. You think Watts is new?"

"There have been white people who tried to help you," Ted interrupted. Joseph sat up, his head bent, and laughed as if sharing a joke with himself.

"Slave owners, White and Uncle Tom cops have been busting our heads since that first half dead and bewildered African landed. There's a brother busted right this moment, whether it's Watts, Buffalo, Birmingham, your call. It's just this time, nobody sucked it in and smiled. And it's going to happen again and again until they don't call it a riot anymore."

"Amen to that Ronnie," Joseph said through a yawn. "Amen. The brothers are turnin' over cop cars and breakin' down some doors." He drank again and gargled a laugh, squinting in surprise at Ted, as if the distance across the table was further than he'd realized.

Ted was leaning as far forward as the rocker would allow. "Compassion. Gandhi, Mr. King? But you want to skip the world, shut us out."

"Read Elijah and Malcolm."

"I have. That's what I'm saying. White Devils. Shut all of us out."

81

Ronnie shook his head. "Pride, man. It's about pride. Bailing out of the white man's habits. Look around you at the post office. I do. What do I see? Less and less Blacks smoking White trash and dropping acid on breaks. Less going after White women. Cleaning ourselves up. Shunning the habits you taught us."

Ted settled back in the rocker. The upper half of his body was outside the tight ring of light from the floor lamp.

"Cats are doin' it." Joseph coughed violently for a moment and was quiet.

"Brother Joseph, I came over because now's the time to stay tight. Close the doors and celebrate your Blackness." Ronnie got up and stretched. "You don't have to become a Muslim. I'm not. Just get tight with your brothers and sisters. Now more than ever, man. Filmore could be burnin' next. Hunter's Point. Where would you be, with this flax on your hands?"

Joseph got up stiffly and looked around uncertainly as if in a place he'd never been. He followed Ronnie out of the light and down the attic to the stairs. They descended. Ronnie's final words were muffled. "Joseph, my Brother, get it together. Dump all this White man's garbage, the flax, booze. Embrace yourself, man. You know what's she's doing to you? She's going...." Their words became an incoherent mumble and died in the sound of a city garbage truck making its stops along the 5 a.m. streets.

Ted jerked open the broad window. The clang of the cans and the truck's engine came in full on the cool, wet air. He dragged the rocker over, sat down abruptly and leaned forward,

82

almost into the dawn, breathing in the freshness, his elbows on his knees, fingers massaging his eyes and temples as he gazed into the new light, watching it slowly brighten until he heard the stairs creak. Footsteps.

Joseph's hands gently squeezed his shoulders. Ted didn't move as he heard him hit the table with his knee and fall back into one of the gullies of the couch. "Anna's listenin' to the news. Watt's still on fire. Burnin'. Don't sound like any let up soon."

Ted had stopped around five last night at Mo's, the neighborhood bar, and watched the news. Most of the pictures were from the sky, helicopters drifting across the night like a chorus of heat seeking insects after prey. Below were the figures standing, running, screaming, shouting, waving hands and clubs, sometimes guns and rifles; they were all silhouette, faceless bobbles in the back light from cars and flaming storefronts. He saw only surfaces, plains of black and grey that had no identity in rage or joy, resignation or revenge, victory-defeat. It was all as if the sound had suddenly been cut away from a motion picture, and you were left to follow along as best you could, trying to make sense of it, thinking you were. Convincing yourself you were. But not really. "The fires?"

Joseph bent forward to reach a jelly jar. "Burnin' everywhere. Even outside Watts. All over L.A."

"Ronnie?"

"Split. He's gotta work at 6:30. Said he'd roll by the Filmore and see what's shakin' before he reports." Joseph lit another cigarette, dropping the flaming wooden match on the floor. It burnt itself out. "The cat is heavy. Almost got his

83

Master's degree in Sociology or somethin' from S.F. State."
Joseph looked at the rafters. "Heavy," he repeated almost
reverently.

"He reads a lot. I've seen him in the library at Berkeley
a couple times."

"Knows history and philosophy, Black and White, all
that shit backwards and forwards. Read all the heavy dudes:
Socrates, Kant, Marx, all those cats. Knows a lot more than
most a them fag professors Anna 'n me hang out with
sometimes. They don't know shit. Ronnie says they only
educated the White man's way."

Ted was half listening as he watched a young fog pass
over the old and ragged Victorians across the street. Lights were
coming on in bedrooms and hallways and going off on the wide
wooden front steps and porches as if by the ghostly hand of the
city's first gas lamplighters. "He's real intense."

"Yeah. You know how the old brothers are at work.
But the young ones dig him."

"Sure, some do." Joseph's head had tilted mechanically
to the left and his eyes were barely open. His cigarette had
become a long ash with the fire close to his fingers. "Hey, watch
it!"

Joseph snorted as his eyes blinked open and he managed
to flick the cigarette into the jelly jar. "Shit." His head lay back
again into the couch, like a passenger unwillingly asleep against
the wooden bench of a bus terminal.

The garbage truck's whine was blocks away now. Once
in a while a car or motorcycle would start up, then drift onto a

84

main street and become one with the city's early morning traffic. "That cat's all right." Joseph's head swayed.

Ted looked beyond Joseph into the emerging outline of the far rafters. "You. You ever think…." His voice trailed off as if it wasn't worth the effort.

Joseph opened his eyes and pulled himself into a sitting position. It was hard since the couch was so deformed and uneven. "What, man?"

"Oh, the way he talks about Anna."

"Cat gotta right to his opinion." Joseph's lips flattened into a resigned smile.

"But she's…."

"My old lady." Joseph's head rotated abruptly towards the rear of the loft.

Anna had come so quietly up the stairs that neither had heard her. Walking without her usual grace, she managed to reach the back of the couch. Only her arms entered the light as her fingers touched Joseph's shoulders and began a gentle massage. "Oh, Yeah." His head titled back toward the shadow of her face. "Oh, yeah, baby."

Though still close to the window, Ted has swiveled the rocker around to face them. "He demeans Anna."

"Joseph and I have a pact," Anna's voice came through the semi-darkness.

"Yeah." Joseph shook his head emphatically, lifting a jar and holding it with both hands as he drank. He carefully lowered it two handed to the table. But as he let go, it toppled. There was only a trickle of red wine left and it lapped up against a fresh Lucky Strike half out of its pack. Joseph ignored it and leaned back to reach up and run his fingers across her wrists and forearms.

"We're going to stand together, whatever happens," Anna exclaimed, interlocking the fingers of her right hand with Joseph's. "Isn't that right, Love?"

Ted got up. "Think I'll drop down to Hanson's for some breakfast.'

Joseph blinked into the light and smiled. "Thanks for droppin' by, mah man."

Ted avoided looking into the dimness for her face as he passed the couch and stove. He reached the hall stairs and ascended with the quick, jaunty step of a boxer. By the time his feet touched the granite front steps he knew she would be standing in front of Joseph while he untied her bathrobe.

The morning air was soft and fresh as he walked to the corner and down the hill to the business district. The fires of Los Angeles would no doubt burn throughout the day.

Mac and Jesus

It was right after P. DeWayne Ditts, Pastor of Operations and Education, had laid down the law and left that Hans, the new Head Custodian, gave me this cruel Hitler Youth smile and said, "Ve ain't going to do a goddamn ting!" followed by laughter that combined a grunt with a cackle. We were sitting in the janitor's room in the basement of the huge old Life New Way Church up near the top of Market Street where the trolleys go through the Twin Peaks tunnel. P. DeWayne had just given me, Hans's new assistant, a tour of the place.

The main sanctuary must hold three thousand people under a dome ceiling painted with fluorescent looking purple-white angels flying in a shaft of light towards Moses standing on a mountain top holding not the tablets but the Gospel for Life New Way version of the Bible and a primitive looking hammer and saw. Dozens of adoring animals of just about every species you could name surrounded him. Later, it was all explained to me, but I never quite got it; New Wavers believe that Moses and Noah was the same person, along with other variations from the Old and New Testament. Below Moses-Noah, way down at the bottom of this treeless and plantless mountain, was John baptizing Jesus in a grey fluorescent river that flowed directly from its base. P. DeWayne's tour also included the attached three story building with its class and meeting rooms painted a color like dried urine on sandstone. The offices behind the main sanctuary housed five full time secretaries and pastors. I was introduced to all, including Head Pastor, J.P. Balthazar.

He was a shake-your-hand-and-grab-your-shoulder kind of guy. His smile was as broad as his round, pale, heavily jowled face under a head of orange hair whose tight curls fringed up over and around a set of flap-sized ears. Except for the fact that it was orange, he and P. DeWayne had identical mustaches. These were pencil thin and didn't so much run parallel with their upper lips as at forty-five degree angles, looking like a pried open V to make room for the nose. Pastor's office was a law partner's dream: Oriental rugs, walls paneled in dark cherry to match the desk and a wall of glass-enclosed book cases. P. DeWayne said that it and the attached private bathroom were, next to the sanctuary and its baptismal tank, our top janitorial priorities.

The tour ended just around the corner from the bathroom. There at the end of a long red carpeted hall leading to the offices were two doors about six feet apart. There was a fluorescent figure of Moses-Noah on the first and one of Jesus on the second. We went through the closest, Moses-Noah, into a short dank hallway whose walls seemed to be painted like river rocks. At the end was a sharp right turn onto a small platform with two steps down into the baptismal tank. A few feet directly across from us was an identical platform and steps. On the wall between and facing the sanctuary flowed another identical fluorescent river whose grey water looked as cold and forbidding as the one on the ceiling.

As P. DeWayne explained it, "Pastor comes this way and the blessed convert from over there" which would have been from the Jesus door side. We stepped, somewhat in unison, down the two steps and took two more to the left into the tank, which put us out in the main sanctuary, down and stage right of the pulpit. We were standing in a six by six foot enclosure whose stucco insides were painted sky blue. Its rim was thick mahogany, stained burgundy like the pews. Somebody had thrown a candy wrapper in the tank along with a decayed apple core, and he picked them both up and wrinkled his nose in disgust. The mustache closed and opened under it and he sighed like a frog might, landing on a banana peel instead of a lily. Then his smile returned and he pressed my arm. "Looka here." I followed his hand across the sanctuary's vaulted ceiling, along the balcony and downstairs to velvet covered pews and, finally, back to me. P. DeWayne turned slightly and raised both arms, pointing toward the river coming down the wall behind us into the tank.

"This is the Holy River Jordan, Bill."

"I thought the Ganges was the holy river."

"Ah'm talkin' about God's river, the river where Jesus, the only son of God, was baptized by John." He paused, frowning until he could see I understood. "The Ganges is a river of idols. There is no idol worship in this Christian church. The Jordan and its holy water cleanse such things away. When you and Hans fill this tank it becomes an extension of that river, flowin' by every third Sunday of the month. And you'll see the power of conversion, right here. You will know what I'm talkin' about."

Hans and I talked about that after P. DeWayne left us to wait for Arnie, an elderly, retired convert who had been trying to help out after the previous custodians left the same day a week ago. It was clear that "left" meant alcohol, because after my interview, P. DeWayne confessed that of the twenty he'd interviewed he was sure I was the only non-alcoholic. He apparently sized up Hans the same. Anyway, Hans's only comment was, again, "Ve ain't going to do a goddamn ting. What? Dat tank? Ve turn on at noon after der service and you

89

turn off at six or seven. Den ve let sit half hour 'til shit and dust come to top and ve skim. Easy. Hell, you tink I got time to worry this place? I work night shift mechanic job at airport and maybe two, three weeks they make me foreman, pay me some money. Then I dump dis shit. Until den, ve just pretend. You tink Mercedes-Benz mechanic got time for dis crap?"

Unlike my new immigrant boss, I did. I guess the logic of most employers who paid real money went like this; with two semesters to complete for your degree, you'll probably be leaving us soon. But they were wrong. They just never believed me when I told them I didn't know when, if ever, I'd go back. Higher education had been a river I'd been floating on and jumping in and out of for years. New majors came and went like dead stars, bright from a distance, then fading the closer you got. At least, as I watched Hans throw me another Hitler Youth smile, he knew where he was headed. For the moment I almost envied him. That changed quickly.

The whole morning consisted of Hans arguing with or belittling Arnie, a dear old man who meant no harm with the smooth, pink, slightly crooked face of an angel, stooped and limping slightly in his careful navigated steps. He had to be nearly eighty, and Hans just had to compete with him. "Jah, jah, you don't need to tell me dat. I know all dat," as if Arnie's mere presence, struggling up and down stairs, breathing hard, meticulously checking his duty roster, was a waste of Hans's time. I was scheduled to work half day and was grateful to leave, figuring if we weren't "going to do a goddamn ting" I'd have lots of time to read. It was compensation for having to work minimum wage with an asshole.

The next day at eight, P. DeWayne was waiting. "Mista Guenther was fired last evenin'."

"That was quick."

"Well...the fireworks began not long after you left. That man." P. DeWayne shrugged and pushed at his mustache with a thumb. "You have never heard such language in your life. And with all the secretaries *and* two ladies considering conversion present!"

"What was he swearing about?" I asked without having to be told.

"Why, poor Arnie. He called that old gentleman every foul name you can think of. Some I'd never heard, but I'm told they were foul. Believe me, after seminary I did some rough housing in graduate school when I got my Masters in Psychology, so I thought I'd heard everything. He actually foamed at the mouth." I tried to imagine Hans's mouth opening and closing like a can of shaving cream, pumping out profanities, the foam spewing forth, then floating gently onto the Oriental rugs. "As you can imagine, I put a stop to that right then. I told him in no uncertain terms that nobody was going to swear in front of our ladies, let alone in the house of God." He paused. "I'd like to offer you the head custodian job." His smile was impish, as if he'd always wanted to.

"I appreciate the offer, Pastor Ditts, but it's really more hours than I want to work."

"I'm sorry, but I do understand." He smiled in resignation, his mustache folding and opening as he did. "Well, I can tell you, I'm not looking forward to interviewing more winos."

Actually, it didn't take as long as either of us probably figured it would, because by mid-morning two days later I was having coffee in the janitor's room when he came down and introduced me to the new Head Custodian. His name was Shawn McGrady, but couldn't remember anybody ever calling him anything but 'Mac.' "Shoot, even my girlfriends used to call me that." Though his black hair was thinning a little up front, it was still thick and curly, running down just a little over his ears into broad sideburns flared at the bottom, and it seemed to continue to move side to side even when, as now, he stopped shaking his head. If his head had been a voice, his hair was the echo, and the way he shook it was not so much side to side, but up and down like a kid being asked if he wanted more ice cream, wondrously wide eyed and smiling. "They always said 'Mac' over the loud speaker when I scored a touchdown in high school. Never my real name like other guys. The damnedest thing." That's when he first shook his head, as if there was wonder in recall, as if there was something back there to be learned that he'd somehow missed.

"What'd you play?"

"Wasn't that good. Sometimes fullback, sometimes half." He walked around the confusion of the janitor's room as he talked. Crap was everywhere: there were stained toilet seats, broken and thrown in one corner, the desk was piled high with miscellaneous junk from a half-eaten, nearly petrified doughnut to rusted tools, to piles of unused note paper looking like it was close to becoming parchment. Mac's face went from a healthy ruddy to red and back as he reviewed our territory. Then he sat down across from me on a barrel of wax. "What happened to the other guy?"

"Guiness Book of Records. He lasted two days." I smiled.

"How about you?"

I leaned back in the scruffy wooden chair and put my feet on the desk's one small vacant spot. "This is day four for me. I needed a job and I've got too much education but not enough to get a good one."

"College boy, huh?" I nodded. "You ever do this kind of work?"

"I've done gardening, janitorial, longshore, bartending, lots of jobs. But I'm not too mechanical, I don't think."

Mac bobbed his head in his special way. "Hell, it's all in doing." He leaned over and opened the supply closet next to him. Half a dozen rolls of toilet paper rolled out onto our cement floor followed by a falling broom that had nothing left of it but a few stiff and blackened bristles. "Fuckin' A," he laughed. "Holy, oh shit, you gotta help me. I made some promises to myself when I took this job. A big one is to stop swearing. I was in the military, see, and it's a habit like smoking. Which I'm not gonna give up. But I want to get rid of the cursing all the time, especially here, a church, a holy place." He was dead serious. "So, just remind me when I start, okay?" I agreed and he stood up. "Had my own janitorial business for a while." He swept the donut off the desk into the trash can. "Lost it though. Christ! Sorry. This place is a pit."

"The guy you replaced told me, "Ve ain't going to do a goddamn ting.'" He laughed. "He had a night job too, big time mechanic."

"Well, I'm gonna tell you straight, Bill, this'll be a piece of cake once it's organized. But until then, we'll be busting our asses..oh, shit...there I go."

93

I didn't much like hearing that because, frankly, I just wanted to loaf, given our measly salaries. So I got up reluctantly. "Look, they're paying us zip."

He raised his hand. It was big and broad like his face and covered with calluses and little nicks where he'd cut himself. "Pay ain't it. You work for the brand or you move on."

"What do you mean?"

"That's cowboy talk. A brand, right? Cattle? We either give it all we got or find another ranch."

I sighed. "How long you figure this will take to get organized?"

"We can square the whole fucking…" I raised my index finger, which became my way of reminding him. "Yeah, we can square the whole place away in maybe a month." He looked at the cement ceiling which was a yellowish-tan, testimony to past janitors breaking Ditts's 'no smoking' rule. "Then we can make a check list of all the little shit…stuff, that's been neglected. We prioritize and go from there." He walked over and gave me a pat on the back, gentle but firm, like a coach sensing talent but lack of enthusiasm and commitment.

There was nothing I wanted less than being a gung-ho janitor in some fringe version of Christianity: Moses and Noah the same person? What next? All I wanted to do was as little as possible, think about Kari, the girl I'd lived with who'd walked out to live with a mutual friend, sit by the dark picture window in my tiny studio watching the city from just above the Twin Peaks Tunnel, and drink a beer or some wine in the company of a joint or cigarette while I tried to figure out where I was going next, except to bed alone.

When I looked up, Mac was back in the center of the room nodding that childlike nod. Then it stopped, the broad smile and high cheek bones falling just enough to become serious. He walked slowly around, talking, adjusting items as he went, stopping every so often to glance or look directly at me. "You know, Bill, you're probably wondering what some fifty year old fart, sorry, is doing working for fifty cents over minimum wage. Well, I could look at you and wonder the same." I started to defend myself but his hand went up again. "No, I started this, and that's your personal business." He tossed a rusted screw driver into a trash barrel. "I may be out of line but let's face it, we gotta work together, whether we like this crapper...oh,oh..or not." He plopped down on the wax can and leaned against the rusted locker behind him. "I'm here 'cause I just came off a six-month bender. You know what Antabuse is? It's a drug they put you on to keep you off booze. They make you take a little and then give you a shot of whiskey. You all of a sudden get so sick you think you're gonna puke your guts and liver and intestines out. And," he laughed, "you almost fucking, ah, almost do. Man, does it make you sick. So you get the message real fast."

"Anyway, in my time of being more than my ordinary stupid, I lost the janitorial business. Me and Carol, my wife, started it a couple years ago when I shipped over from the Marines. Good money plus my thirty year pension. Don't think we didn't work our fannies...that's not a curse...off." He picked up a note pad that looked like it had been used for toilet paper and slammed it into the trash. "What an asshole." He ignored my raised finger. "I get a good thing going and always seem to blow it."

"How's your wife taking all this, if you don't mind my asking?"

"She's a damn saint, still loves me, no matter how stupid I get. It's 'causa her and the Bible I'm here." He waved his hand as if swatting at a fly that had buzzed his forehead. "I just wanted you to know. That's why I gotta make this place work out for me. Come on, let's get goin'."

Though I went into it kicking and screaming, it was next to impossible not to get caught up in Mac's energy. That first day we took everything out of the janitorial room, scrubbed it with soap and hot water, floor to ceiling, desk, lockers, cabinets, threw out enough junk to almost fill the dumpster, and painted everything white and the floor gun metal grey. With two coats to dry, we couldn't move back in for a week, but it had a whole new feeling when we did.

By early afternoon two days later, we had waxed and buffed the wood floors in the main entry and hallways in both buildings, and vacuumed the main sanctuary including every velvet pew cushion. Mac, against my protest, convinced P. DeWayne that we should start at seven instead of eight to be sure the offices shined before anybody arrived. Sitting in my dark studio that evening, after three hours of OT, *without pay,* I could barely conjure up a single moment of the past with Kari before I put the half-finished beer away and slept like the dead for the first time in months.

Other than having to work so hard, the only major drawback was running into pastors and church volunteers and employees in the halls. They invariably said things like, "Jesus blesses your work," or "Let the tablet bearer and arc builder be your guide."

96

One afternoon I could hear Mac in a semi-intense discussion with P. DeWayne on the landing between the two buildings as I lugged mop, pail, cleaner and wax to the third floor class rooms. Mac was trying hard to grasp the Moses-Noah idea. He'd told me he thought it was some kind of key to his understanding. P. DeWayne was losing his patience, because Mac had such a hard time with it all. About an hour later he came up to get me.

There was a hole in the wall, about a ten stool and five booth diner just across the street, and we went over for coffee, our first real break in three weeks. On the first stool by the window Mac sat smoking and looking out at Market Street traffic, never once looking at me as we talked. "So, Bill, what do you figure on stuff like this Moses and Noah thing?"

"Sounds a little strange to me, Mac."

"Now don't be so college boy quick about it. Who's to say their version of the Bible is off?"

"A couple thousand years of Christianity?"

"Yeah, but maybe there was a mistake. Maybe somebody translated something all wrong." He sipped some coffee and lit another cigarette. "If they are crazy, how come the congregation's so big? Hell fire, twenty-five hundred people or more on average for Sunday service. Ten to twenty Sunday night conversions or regular baptisms a month with another, say, couple thousand attending those."

"Mac, it's San Francisco, 1968. You have any idea how many phony swamis, pastors and gurus have come through town since 'The Haight' took off in '63?"

97

A grunt acknowledged my point. But it didn't convince him. "It's gotta mean something. Look at Ditts and Pastor Balthazar and the rest. Sometimes I figure they're a whole lot happier than us."

"I would be too if I was making what I should be for all the work we're doing, instead of minimum wage."

"Don't be cynical. I think, well, I do think the Lord led us both here for a reason. I do."

"If He buys this Moses-Noah idea he must be happy with the way we're shining up his place of worship."

Mac gave me the 'kid wanting more ice cream' nod with that wide open Irish smile and punched my shoulder. "Let's finish waxing that top floor today."

And for two solid months that's how it went, checking off another priority every few days from the list we kept on a clipboard hung inside our door. But even with all that we accomplished, it never seemed enough for P. DeWayne. While the secretaries and members were full of compliments, P. DeWayne always had some small item, as small as a trash can unemptied, that he'd drop on us in his wispy, off-handed way. It drove Mac up the wall. "That damn little weasel. That front lobby, every classroom and hall, we got 'em shinin' like a nigger's heel, and I'll bet you Ditts would white glove the floor some Sunday right after church, foot traffic and all, and show us the dust he found!"

"Not much Christian charity in P. DeWayne, Mac."

"No, now, I don't mean that. He's a real Christian all right."

"How can you tell?"

"There you go again, Bill."

"I'm only asking."

"Yeah, but I can see that little hidden smile a yours." I had to admit it. "See. Look, I know 'cause he kind of confides in me. A few days ago he told me about the seminary, how hard it was for him." We were down in the basement kitchen. It opened onto a huge dining-assembly area with a stage at one end. Must have been a hundred fifty feet by a hundred twenty. We'd just finished painting the walls and ceiling a creamy pink at the request of the church's interior decorations committee. With the lights turned low and all the camp tables and metal chairs out, it looked like a cross between the entrance to Dante's inferno--hot, glossy and foreboding--and the dance floor of some cowboy bar in Fresno. We were doing much neglected projects now. This one was tearing down a grease infested Wolfe commercial stove and cleaning every last part in the triple metal sinks. "He said most of them sectarians...."

"Seminarians?"

"Yeah. Most of 'em use to buy a different boy-girlie porno magazine every week, smuggle it in and have a circle jerk late Sunday nights in the shower." He waved off my laughter. "No, he was real serious. 'Course he didn't call it a circle jerk, or even masturbation. Said it was, let's see, 'sinnin in the shower'."

"Like singing?"

99

Mac ignored that. "Said he'd prayed for hours afterwards for God to keep those pictures of naked couples humpin,' that he'd peeked at, out of his head."

"That's rugged. He was a real St. Francis, maybe even a Buddha."

"There you go, judging. Judge not, remember the Bible." He was studying it every day now, the original version. "It *was* rugged for Ditts, that's the point." I nodded. He was right, and I felt his compassion, whether misplaced or not. "It's like what I'm doing, sort of, staying off booze."

"You've done terrific, Mac." He had.

"Thanks, but I got a long ways to go." He tore back into the stove.

We'd worked for about two hours when suddenly, Grace, Pastor Balthazar's secretary, appeared on the stairs outside the kitchen windows. She was moving as fast as her brittle eighty-five pound body would allow, her ankle length flowered dress billowing as if empty as she came down a few steps and screamed, "It's Pastor Maravell!"

Hurrying up the stairs, we doubled back along its iron railing to the 'Pastor's Door,' a door used only by them next to the row of reserved parking stalls with names on brass plates against the church wall. Unfortunately, in her panic Grace had closed that door. It was the only one to which we didn't have a key.

"Holy jumpin' Jesus!" Mac pounded with his open hand on the iron door, ignoring my raised index finger. Almost instantly Grace opened it and we ran past Pastor Balthazar's

100

private toilet, then left along the hall where the baptismal doors were and toward the offices. From far away came the sound of excited whispers punctuated by frequent and nearly hysterical pleas from Pastor Balthazar, "Oh, dear God!" and "Lord, save thy brother in Christ!"

Mac burst into the office lobby in front of me. "Anybody call for an ambulance?" They nodded in unison. Pastor Maravell lay flat on his back alone on the far side of the Oriental rug by his office door. His huge head patched with spots of long straw and grey colored hair was still, but his right arm kept thrusting back and forth across his massive stomach and receding chest as if trying to roll over or rise up. There in the rich colors of the carpet, his three hundred pounds with its almost pear shaped head and spare hair pattern seemed to be struggling like an old whale trapped on the shallow thorns of a coral reef.

Mac was giving me on the spot instructions in CPR as if only the two of us were in the room. He positioned the head slightly tilted back, and, though it disgusted me, Mac seemed hardly aware of the saliva and mucus that he dug out and pulled away from the white, bulbous lips before he went mouth to mouth with Pastor Maravell. Then he'd stop and motion to me, my hands on the slope of his chest that fell from neck to stomach as I clumsily tried to gain a foothold and rhythm, pumping near what I hoped was his sternum. Twice Pastor Balthazar called from across the rug, but Mac ignored him, going mouth to mouth again. Pastor Maravell finally let out a sigh followed by a blaring fart as his eye lids fluttered, opened and he was breathing on his own.

When the paramedics arrived, we had him half erect, and he was able to stand before they settled him onto the gurney the office staff and pastors followed out to the ambulance. Mac stopped in Pastor Balthazar's toilet to wash and rinse his mouth. "Suppose this is off limits too," he grinned.

"You did special duty."

When we returned to the basement, we stood just outside the kitchen door and smoked. "Maybe a mild heart attack." The smoke steamed down through his nostrils. "That much fat, it's just a matter of time."

"Where'd you learn all that?"

"I did eighteen years in the Corps as a platoon sergeant, then decided to switch to being a medic because my knees were starting to go. Did that my last twelve." He motioned us back inside where the stove awaited like a greasy monolith.

"You must have helped a lot of people in Vietnam."

"It was all just gettin' into gear then. The villages got hit hardest. Lots a civilian dead. Don't know how much help we were there, because they never trusted us. So, you'd get 'em when whatever they had was usually close to out of control." He paused, the wire brush in his hand resting on the upturned grill. Mac stared out the window as if trying to see clearly a distant image. Finally he started in again with the brush. "There was a little girl."

"Was she okay?"

"Yeah, guess so."

"What'd she have?"

"Nothin'," He stopped and looked at me. The sky blue eyes were asking a question, but I didn't know what it was. "It doesn't matter."

"What?"

"There's a lot of sinnin' to make up for." He glanced into the gutted stove as if it were a cauldron of the sins he'd committed, or imagined he'd committed.

"Huh? You just saved someone's life and turned this church from a dump into a diamond."

"So what? There's a lot I gotta make up for, pay for, like putting Carol through all this shit, stuff. It was a sign from God to let me be here."

"You think you'll join?"

He grunted. "Hell, I don't know. Carol doesn't buy this Moses and Noah as one guy deal."

"No kidding?"

He gave me a quick glance. "Like I told you, look at how they're doing. You see anybody here looks like they could use a meal? What about their cars? Their clothes? What the hey, you can count the old cars at Sunday service on one hand." His big right paw pushed back through the thick hair a couple of times. Mac used to do this whenever he was suspicious or when he didn't have a clue as to what something really meant.

About a week later P. DeWayne flew into the janitor's room in such a high state of excitement that Mac and me, at least me, eating our lunch at the time, thought he'd just seen Jesus, or at least Moses-Noah. By now we'd cleaned and painted the

103

furniture white, including the old desk. It may have been windowless, but it has become for me the brightest room in the church.

"Dear Lord, I have been so remiss that, gentlemen, I must beg your forgiveness."

"What's up, Pastor?" Mac asked half way through a banana.

"It's the 12th Annual Mission Festival. Somehow it wasn't on my calendar and Pastor Balthazar just reminded me. We're holding it here in this assembly room a week from this coming Saturday."

"What's the festival?"

"Why nothing less than a gathering of Life New Way Missionaries from around the world." P. DeWayne pinched his lips into such a tight, gleeful smile that the sides of his mustache nearly vanished into each other. "I apologize because, well, starting Monday bright and early we're gonna help arriving missionaries set up their booths, arrange chairs, displays, just about everything."

It was a week in hell. The missionaries who appeared gracious enough when introduced quickly became a basement full of shouting, demanding desires and commands that we were supposed to instantly fulfill without regard for what Mac or me were doing or whether or not we were helping their fellow missionaries. It was everything from masking tape to nails, hammers to batteries, donuts to sandwiches, none of which were received with so much as a 'thank you.'

On Friday, the final day of preparation, we retreated to the hole in the wall across the street for lunch. Mac slumped down, elbows and forearms on the counter, shook his head like a horse shaking off fleas. "Man, I don't know what I want to do most: eat, go get a drink or punch out one ah them." His thumb jerked toward the church, now far away across Market Street and emerging from a morning fog.

Pashudi, the Indian proprietor, delivered up two greasy cheeseburgers, onion rings and real ice cream vanilla malts. "Chreestians!" he exclaimed in his clipped Hindu-British accent.

"Christians?" Mac's first bite devoured a major portion of the burger and he crammed an onion right in behind it. "If I was to walk in there right now with Jesus," he exclaimed amidst the chews, "I'll bet he couldn't find a one."

"Moses-Noah!" Pashudi interjected. He and Mac were like a couple of foreigners who couldn't understand a word the other was saying. Mac just belched.

Half an hour later, we trudged back to help with the finishing touches. I left Mac at six. I felt a little guilty about it, but we'd worked long hours for no overtime pay, and we were due back at six the next morning to mop, sweep and buff the basement which still managed to look like a cowboy bar despite the booths overflowing with religious décor.

By the time I had showered and finished some soup with a glass of wine and a cigarette, the ex-girlfriend was only a figment of my imagination. Laying on the bed, I realized that for going on three months now I'd been working harder than ever, except the summer of my junior year when I did an internship at a legal aid storefront over in the Filmore District. There, I had worked from 7 a.m. to 7 or 8 p.m., six days a week and never got paid a dime, except meals. Yet I'd loved the feeling of exhaustion at day's end after maybe ten hours doing research at the law library or writing intake complaints from people who were dead-helpless in a system where usually only money buys rights and protection. Maybe it was just the sense of exhaustion and accomplishment that went with it that made me remember; janitors did the same in their way. I was asleep before I could figure out whether or not I believed that.

For reasons unknown, the guy downstairs had forgotten to open the trash door, and at four-thirty by my clock I came stark awake with the banging and shouting of two garbage men. They made enough sustained noise to assure I wasn't going back to sleep. So, at five-thirty, with a freshly baked sweet roll and large coffee from the local bakery, I walked the last dark, long block down Market Street and under the neon sign extending over the side walk, "Gospel for Life New Way Church—Rejoice!"

Peering in the basement door, I had the feeling something was wrong; there were no lights on, which was the opposite of what it was supposed to be. I knew there was something wrong when I closed the door and heard the wall heater nearby purring away; P. DeWayne's strict orders were no heat on overnight. In the darkness, the burner flames reflected off the polished wood floors and up against the creamy pink walls and ceiling, blending with the first imperceptible blush of dawn above the lines of missionary booths standing like an abandoned circus midway. Then I saw Mac's head.

He lay on his back on the floor within inches of the heater, and the blue-yellow flame's reflection seemed to dance excitedly around him like Lilliputians keeping watch. Not a sound but the flames. I knelt on both knees and stared at the broad, fleshy face and strong neck until his head moved and he saw me. "Hey, shee. Bill. Galdim it. Sombitch." I helped him struggle to a sitting position. Mac rubbed his eyes and blinked vigorously. "Holy, sweet Jesus," he moaned, "did it to myself again!"

"Mac, it's okay. There's nobody here."

"I stayed 'til near eleven, sweeping and the rest. Then called Carol. Said, sleep here. She was pissed. I got a half pint. Crap." He stretched back and pulled the bottle from behind the heater. Cheap whiskey, capped and nearly empty.

"What about the Antabuse?"

"I went off it a week ago. Figured I was gonna make it this time. I was doin' so good, and just when I'm doin' good I screw up again." He scrambled to his feet and half fell against the wall for support. "Gotta do a last minute check out."

"I'm driving you home. There's time for me to get back before anyone arrives. I'll tell P. DeWayne you hurt your back last night."

"No, I gotta…."

"Bullshit." Under protest, I wrestled him to his VW Bug and we drove to the avenues.

On the way he stared out into the early fog, grimacing and shaking his head from time to time. "See, what I told ya? Mac, sinner, no matter what. No matter I been reading the Bible, trying. Sometimes I think it ain't no use; Devil's got me by the short hairs, period."

107

"You have to stop thinking like that. You sound like I do sometimes." He squinted at me. "I'm saying, you can stop that crap way of being."

The open window letting in the cool approaching ocean air and winter morning had sobered him enough that he wasn't slurring now. "Now, can't think a nothin' done right 'cept that little girl in 'Nam...maybe a few others too." He stared blankly out the window. "Had one a them rasty jungle infections, a good two inches in diameter around her elbow, right down to the bone, and some a the ugliest blue-black skin and tissue you ever saw. Like a burn, a napalm kiss. Shit. At first the Doc who did Sunday medical call with me in the village near us thought it was gangrene. Anyways, two and a half months, every Sunday, she'd come with her Mama. I'd give 'em soap and antibiotics, redress the infection and repeated the same orders to the old lady. And just like some priest doin' his first Communion, she followed 'em. When I left, it was down to a tiny, healthy scab at the tip of her elbow." He motioned to turn on 30th. Like all the others on the block, his place was a small two story butted against a similar one on either side, small lawns, single car garages. He was starting to relax and the booze inched back over him. "I'm, I'm dreamin' a Jesus."

"When?"

"S'morning." He coughed into his red bandanna handkerchief. "He found me where you did and we went wandering through the church. We seen, saw, P. DeWayne praying by the baptismal tank and he, Jesus, opened his arms and blessed him. But Ditts didn't seem to feel it."

"I can imagine." He wasn't listening.

108

"Then, we sat in the front row and he raised his arm toward that river Jordan picture and then looked up and smiled at the ceiling when he saw himself and John and Moses-Noah up there on the dome. We sat down in the front pew. I can't tell you how it felt good, but it did. It was like the world was okay…if you could just trust. Finally, he took me by the hand and we went back and he settled me on the floor again. Jes' before he went away I thought he was laughing at me. Though, maybe he was just smilin'. Or maybe it was just me imagining it all." I pulled into his driveway. "You take the car and come back later. We'll drive you home." He got out stiffly, took out the bottle from his blue Navy coat and put it on the seat. "I owe you, Bill." Mac's gait wasn't bad as he went up the driveway and into Carol's arms. She waved and mouthed 'thank you' over his shoulder to me.

Luckily, P. DeWayne bought my story and the day went pretty smoothly. Even Pastor Balthazar stopped by later when I was leaving and the missionaries were gathering their stuff to go. Told me how good the church looked. Driving back to Mac's, I wondered if he'd be up to opening for Sunday service.

Greeting me at the door, he appeared almost normal except for a bruise on his left cheek where it looked like he slept. Carol came from behind him and hugged me, graciously demanding that I stay for dinner. Though probably worse for wear from the morning, her smile didn't reveal it even in the wrinkle lines that had begun to trickle from her cheek bones down the soft, freckled plain of her face. I wanted to stay, wanted to spend the evening with them and their oldest son, home on leave from the Marines, but it would have been too hard to pretend everything was okay.

Mac and I drove to my place in silence. I didn't want to break it, and had the door open as soon as the engine died. "Bill?"

"Yeah?" He leaned towards me a little as if I couldn't hear.

"You know my dream? Where Jesus looked up at the dome and smiled at himself and John and Moses-Noah?" I nodded. "You think that was some kind a sign to me?"

"Could be, Mac. I wish I could tell you for sure."

"Yeah, just maybe." He stared out the window into the gathering darkness. "Oh, make sure the baptismal's off by six instead of seven tomorrow night, will you? Looks like it'll need a hell of a skimmin'."

"Sure"

"Don't worry. I'll be okay for set up tomorrow."

I got up early the next morning and went down with money I couldn't really spare and had breakfast at my favorite café over on 19th just off Castro. It was a working people's café that served the kind of food my mother made: fresh pies, homemade sausage and buttermilk pancakes with hot, real maple syrup. Afterwards, I cleaned my studio and went through a ritual I'd been doing a lot the past few years. I gathered assorted clothes, furniture and other stuff that I felt was kind of holding me down, weighing on me, and put it all in the Salvation Army storage bin at the market on 19th. Then I showered and lay on the fold out couch until four, staring at the white plaster ceiling and dark wood molding, and listening to the trolleys coming and going through the tunnel below me.

I didn't think about my ex, Kari, the whole time. Images of people and places from the church and from other times like the internship kept intersecting when I'd close my eyes, and just when they were about to collide, they'd vanish. Ron, the legal aid lawyer, had gone to a hot shot Ivy League school which he hated. Said he'd never have become a lawyer if it weren't for the people you got to try and help. But realistically, you mostly couldn't do much. Law was money. I'd wanted to be an Ivy Leaguer. Even got accepted at Harvard but couldn't afford it. The romance and power, I guess. Ron, who wasn't that much older, said it was mostly bullshit. Overhearing some of the church secretary's joke about the pastors and their own jobs and how much they hated them both, I wondered how anybody stuck with anything for long.

At four, I got off the couch and put on my Sunday work clothes: white Oxford button-down, slacks, brown loafers and a crew neck cashmere sweater my folks sent me for Christmas. The mile walk down Market felt good.

There was an eerie silence in the sanctuary when I went up to flip on the lights in the lobby halls. I listened for familiar sounds. The distant urban whisper of a freeway came first, followed by a hiss at the heating vents as the big furnace downstairs rumbled onward. Now and then would come a crack of a pew or wooden beam down in the darkness of the sanctuary in front of me. Only the pulpit was illuminated by a single yellow light from up where the angels were. Jesus, John and Moses-Noah were vague outlines from below. Then it hit me.

I ran down the center aisle in a panic. There was no sound of water pouring into the baptismal. It was dry. Mac had forgotten.

111

Leaping into the tank I turned on the faucet. The water pressure was weak--that was why it took so long to fill--so weak that as it dribbled into the darkness at my feet I wondered why it just didn't evaporate before hitting bottom. I hurried to the front office and called Mac. He answered on the second ring. There was music and laughter in the background.

"Hi, Bill." He wasn't drunk, just a little mellow. Where was Carol? "It's her birthday. A little party, a few friends. Don't worry, I'm fine."

"Mac, there's no water in the tank."

"What!?" It sounded like he nearly dropped the phone. "Goddamn it. Christ on a bleeding toboggan! I really screwed it this time. I'm...I'm on my way." The phone went dead before I could protest.

I didn't do anything. Just sat waiting in the front pew with the lights off. We had about two hours before anybody arrived because, maybe luckily, I had decided to come in even earlier since it took so long to skim. The tank might be above your knees by then. Even if by some miracle we got it filled, there'd be no "skim time." I had to smile. It would be the church's first dry baptism service.

But Mac, arriving in record time, had other ideas. He squinted into the tank, then signaled for me to follow him out to the pastor's parking lot entrance and down the outside basement stairs. We stood for a minute in the dusky kitchen like two thieves who'd searched but found nothing of value.

"Grab a couple waste baskets from our room," he finally stammered.

The ones I came up with were the cleanest I could find, but this was no time to be particular. God, Moses-Noah, or whomever was either with us or not as we began lugging cans of water up the stairs into the pastor's entrance and straight through the sacred doors into the tank. Fortunately, we'd had the presence of mind to lay down the rubber matting on the carpets the day before, because on my first trip up I realized that Mac and I, staggering under the weight of water filled waste baskets, were depositing about a third of our load on the stairs, parking lot, and on the rubber mat.

But we kept at it for an hour and a half, going as fast as the water pressure allowed. Fortunately for us, the downstairs was on a different line with a little more pressure. Pastor Balthazar was the first to arrive, and Mac explained how there'd been a plumbing problem. It was just after that Mac had a brighter idea. Grabbing the garden hose with an adaptor, we hurried up to Pastor Balthazar's toilet. Mac didn't bother to knock as he pushed the door open with his shoulder and we stopped dead, staring through the toilet into the pastor's study where he was giving advice to some soon-to-be-marrieds who looked as healthy and rosy as a baby's cheek. All Mac did was give a little bow and say, "Sorry to disturb you folks," before he gently closed the inner door.

It looked as if his idea was going to work, because by plugging into the pastor's sink and turning off the outlet in the tank, we got better pressure from the bathroom sink to the tank. We were going to make it, but, unfortunately and as predicted, there would be no time for skimming. So when the service began we could only sit anxiously in the dark projection booth in the balcony and watch, hoping for the best.

Pastor Maravell, now back at work and in full voice, was reading from the Life New Way Gospel version of the Bible when the organ thundered a series of introductory notes, and Pastor Balthazar appeared to glide from his side of the tank into the water. He raised his arms toward Pastor Maravell and then towards the dome, like I imagined Jesus did in Mac's dream. The congregation suddenly whispered "Hail to our King!" and fell instantly silent. We watched in horror as Pastor Balthazar glanced briefly at the water, his hand casually pushing what looked to be an orange peel away from himself. His eyes grew narrow as he scanned the sanctuary. Mac ducked, even though he could never have seen our faces that high up and pressed against the projection booth window. "Sweet Jesus," Mac gulped. But Pastor Balthazar's steely glance softened into utter beatitude as he took the hand of the first convert and guided her into the tank.

The woman, about Mac's age, was dressed in a white tunic. She looked nearly as big as Pastor Maravell: the thick neck, enormous jowls and broad forehead. Her brown hair was tied tightly in a huge white bow and it resembled the top knot of a Sumo wrestler. If Pastor Balthazar hadn't caught her, she'd have gone down making the final step from her side into the tank.

They struggled, clinging to each other until their balance returned, and the ceremony began. Though we couldn't understand the words, the deep resonant power of Pastor Balthazar's voice boomed against our small spy hole. Finally, he turned toward the new convert. She was smiling through the tremor of her upper body. Even on a good day there was never enough hot water.

114

After a few adjustments and a false start, Pastor Balthazar gently supported the woman as she settled back on his arm. Though he'd done this a thousand times and knew all the lifting techniques, his pinkish red complexion showed the strain.

Somehow he managed to complete the submersion, but then it was hard to tell up where we were just what happened. The woman's powerful pudgy arms shot above her submerged head and then the pastor lost his grip. There was a struggle as her head came up and her hands were dog paddling, slapping the water, until Pastor Balthazar was able to get behind her and began to lift with everything he had, until, finally, she came out of the water with a heave as the congregation let out one simultaneous gasp. Her great breasts shown through the water soaked tunic, and some silver foil or wrapping paper from the tank had wedged into her hair. It glistened like a beat up star as she and Pastor Balthazar, both breathing hard, leaned against the tank. Then the organ boomed again. I turned to say something to Mac. He was gone.

I got to the parking lot just as he was turning the little white VW up Market Street. I ran along the side walk yelling his name like a psycho, "Mac, Mac!" I was sure he heard me but never looked back as the car crested Market and disappeared.

It was strange how little was said about the incident. P. DeWayne once again offered me the Head Custodian job; Mac had called the next day and resigned, refusing his final check, donating it to the church. I tried to call him, even rode the bus out to his house. But nobody was home or ever answered the door.

Old Arnie and I tried our best until P. DeWayne hired a guy who could have been Hans's brother. Instead of saying, "Ve ain't going to do a goddamn ting," he just smiled like an SS officer and said, "Dey get vat dey pay for. Nathing else."

In the months after Mac left, the church, under my new boss, was slowly returning to its neglected state. I tried at first, but it was too much for one person. So I began spending about three hours a day reading books I never read for an Introduction to Constitutional Law course I'd dropped a year before, while the new boss made personal phone calls and smoked. The books were interesting, not that I'll end up doing anything with the law. With money as the prime mover, I think you'd be shoveling the tide back with a teaspoon like my friend from legal aid.

I surprised myself when I decided to quit and get back on the G.I. Bill for summer school. If I stick it out this time, in a year I can wind up with my BA and a double major in English and Sociology. Also, I met this terrific girl not long after Mac left. She lives in a studio smaller than mine over by UC Medical Center near the park, and has just six months left to finish her nursing degree. I told her about Mac and I can tell that she really cares.

Most Sundays when the weather is nice, we take a backpack filled with fruit and water and walk all the way through Golden Gate Park, along the beach, and back. I keep hoping to find Mac under a tree wrestling with the whole Moses-Noah thing, or lying in the grass with his Bible, trying to figure out what Jesus wants him to do next.

Rabbis for Sale or Rent

Almost soundlessly, Ted rode through the edge of morning, that moment before dawn at night's end when the city kept its own silent counsel. Crisscrossing his way downtown through the Filmore District, Pacific Heights, Russian and, finally, Nob Hill, the commute, rain or shine, on the old '55 BMW motorcycle had become a ritual he loved.

Each day the street shared its secrets with him: lamps lit darkened windows like clockwork; the same people touched the sidewalks at the same time, got into the same cars, waited for the first bus or trolley. That early, it was still a small town where people recognized each other because they were few and it was only 4:30 a.m.

He'd bought the motorcycle from someone in his neighborhood who had returned to where he'd come from to pick up where he'd left off. Though he liked the feeling of power the deep bellow of the muffler gave, Ted had installed one whose sound was no louder than the average car, perhaps quieter than some. In a couple hours the silence around him would vanish. It would be a city again.

He sometimes imagined that when he talked to the motorcycle it understood and responded to his gentle touch. They came down Washington Street between the unbroken wall of apartment buildings and turned into the upper yard of the Municipal Railroad's cable car barn and office. He parked behind the welder's shed. Night mechanics were lining up and checking out the first cable cars at the exit gate. They waved but seldom spoke that early.

Ted was the first run of the day, 5:05. It was 4:45. Not even his conductor or the extra board man was in the Gilley Room. Billy Carney, the night dispatcher, motioned him over to the window that divided the office and the crew area. The window was like a movie ticket booth with a counter and slightly larger opening at the bottom of the glass. When first hired, he'd asked Joe Lugano, the chief instructor, what the glass was for. Joe's only answer was, it had been there since the time he'd been hired as a gripman, twenty-six years ago.

Billy bent down to talk. His voice always sounded like he was training it. "Mr. Bailey wants to see you guys at 1:30 when you get relieved."

"Any idea why?"

"You never heard it here." Billy looked at him until he got a Scout's Honor signal from Ted. "Remember those guys Tuesday?"

"Yeah."

"One of 'em filed a bitch."

"Okay. 1:30. The Breeze didn't call in sick or anything?"

"That ever happen?"

Ted smiled and went to his locker where he picked up his gloves and hat. As he walked back out to inspect his cable car, Breeze, his conductor, was coming in. "We have to see Bailey after work about you know who."

Their hands slapped in passing. "Got it, brother. Be out in a flash."

118

With each trip from the gazebo turntable at Aquatic Park to Market Street and back, Ted couldn't get an angle on how he and Breeze ever got to verbally duking it out with the seven Reform Convention rabbis which started at California and Powell and continued all the way to the wharf. Unfortunately, he wasn't any closer to an explanation when they were relieved at 1:25 that afternoon.

Breeze walked back up the hill to the exit gate entrance, but Ted decided to go in the front way. As he climbed the wide stairs to the office, he felt the rumbling vibrations as cable cars above were being returned to and pulled from the barn and onto the tracks in the yard. Where the stairs ended he pushed open the heavy iron door and entered the barn. Rows of the iron and wood cars stood empty and silent, track after track, beneath a mass of high interlocking steel beams, like forgotten toys in the dark and dusty attic of memory, waiting infinitely patient to be hauled out into the light again.

Midday sun had already moved west of the building, leaving the Gilley Room with its east facing windows to fill with ever expanding shadows that covered the benches, lunch tables, the frayed pool table, and rows of employee wall lockers in the rear. Ted put away his hat and gloves. Through the dispatcher's window and office he could see the closed door to Superintendent Chuck Bailey's corner office.

Al Gonzalez, the day dispatcher, called through the glass opening, "He'll be with you in a minute. Talking to Breeze right now."

Ted acknowledged and sat down on one of the lunch tables facing the high windows. He rested his black engineer boots on the bench and stared out. Just how was he going to accurately explain it?

No picture post card shot of the city in October even comes close to what you see when you're there. Always a light breeze in the flags atop the St. Francis Hotel lying back against a Chagall blue sky, cool under a tree out in the park or deep in the Financial District until you step from the shadows into a warmth that never makes you sweat. It was that kind of day.

We'd just come up from Pine and over the hump and coasted in the full sun through noon traffic across California to our stop. The Breeze, real name Jerome Travis, surrounded by tourists on the rear platform, leans against his brake handle just as relaxed as his view is of the bay and the Berkeley hills beyond.

I didn't see it, but I should have. It's how they were waiting, all of them in dark expensive suits in the middle of the street while cabs and cars honk and try to snake past. With everybody else waiting on the curb for us to stop you'd think a light bulb would have gone off? But no. They just stand there like portly Easter Island statues in the shadow of the Fairmont Hotel. Oblivious.

Since all the seats are taken, they jump on the running boards on both sides before I can set the track brake and stop us. From no hats, plastic I.D. badges and the wing tip shoes, they're anybody from Sioux Falls Republicans to Detroit car salesmen at a convention up at the Mark Hopkins or Fairmont. We unload and load and Breeze gives me two bells to go, and we're rolling again down toward the fringe of Chinatown and the upper edge of North Beach.

There's no room on the running boards for the biggest of the group who's about six feet, surrounded by a forty-eight inch waist. He leans against the cabin over my right shoulder between the boarding steps and the inside cabin door. In other words, the guy is smiling at his buddies while taking up all the platform space where major traffic at every stop moves in and out of the main cabin. Could be, I thought, he's the boss, head of the marketing department, taking his guys for lunch up in North Beach. But most likely they'll be with us to the wharf.

"Please, would you move inside? You're blocking the aisle there."

He glances over at me as the car swings into the Jackson curve and we head up to Mason between some very old and pretty run down storefronts and apartments where sometimes the sound of mah-jongg pieces can be heard moving if you walk there in the middle of the night. His group hears this exchange; well, my side of it since he hasn't replied. They poke each other to be sure everybody got it and watch to see what his next move is. It's nothing. No response. He tries to pull his chest up off his stomach and stares out the front window.

At the Mason stop I ask again as Breeze leans past me to pick up the outside bench and running board fares. "Look, you can't stand there. You're blocking the way."

Eyes still straight ahead. Maybe deaf? His buddies are on the verge of a mass smirk. I ease back on the grip and we get momentum as the grip locks onto the cable. As hills go, the one between Mason and Jones on Jackson is about a 6 out of 10 with

1 being the steepest, but its harrowing because the road is so narrow that running board tourists can and have gotten their butts clipped and shoes scraped by cars parked too far from the curb. It's either that or the guy ahead of us, right then, about three quarters of the way up trying to shoe horn a beat up Lincoln into a VW Bug space. I grab the bell cord and try to make us sound like a fire truck in full cry, and we grease past the front bumper by a hair and onto the flat at Jones.

Two regulars, elderly ladies, edge cautiously from the curb toward the front platform. Breeze gets off and takes one on each arm. He starts toward the back but he knows they prefer getting on in front. The guy in the aisle looks glued to the cabin. Breeze hoists the old gals up onto the platform and I help them squeeze between the bench and the stomach and go inside. Before he walks to the rear, Breeze looks up from under the brim of his hat, his eyes unseen behind mirrored sunglasses, like the sudden and possibly terrifying presence of a panther through the undergrowth. "Hey, mah man, where are your manners?"

"Perfectly intact, *man*," says the guy with a wispy smile for his friends who grin back like two rows of frogs on a swamp log.

Ignoring the others, Breeze slowly raises his black gloved hands to his hips and, tapping with the toe of one black Italian boot, he looks our friend over like a USDA inspector seizing up a slab of decayed meat. Then he turns and shoots some bad rays at the rest of the group before walking to the rear platform where he gives me two bells and we take the gentle slope down to Taylor.

There, a young Chinese mother with two kids in crisp and starched parochial school uniforms, also regulars, go through the same routine boarding. The larger of the two, a little boy about seven, trips on the top step and stumbles into the guy's stomach and, I guess, accidentally steps on the wing tips in the bargain. This time he glances menacingly down at the mother. "Madam, get control of those children." She mutters her apologies and cuffs the boy on the shoulder as they enter the cabin.

That tore it for me. I pull the track brake on hard, lean on the grip handle and stare at him. "Although I don't think we have to be nice anymore, let me ask you nicely for the last time. Please move inside so people don't have to fall over you. Or, hang out there with your friends." That caught his attention, slightly. He turns his big head and gives me the once over from the bridge of his nose down, like royalty forced to mingle with the "great unwashed." His face is puffy, forehead set back with a big Roman nose and full lips sticking out as if he'd just pulled a sucker from his mouth. The lips open, moving in and out, a big fish taking on water. Eyes protrude from deep sockets, and I remember a childhood turtle poking his head out. I'm not kidding. Even his hair is weird, a curly black steel wool crushed with heavy oil.

"If you wish to ask me something, you will address me as 'sir'."

"That's right, that's right," chime in the six buddies who have suddenly become a kind of Greek chorus.

"I resent such an attitude as yours." I didn't think I'd made it sound *that* bad.

"We've done this too many times already. You're blocking the doorway. Remember the old ladies, those 'out of control kids' just now?"

The chorus looked at me in disbelief and then at each other. "What a wise guy," one said and the rest nodded. Then in unison, "You don't have to take that, Jacob."

Releasing the brake, I ease forward and we roll down the long slight grade to Hyde. I tried to smile and wave to three skinny Japanese kids playing with a hula hoop in front of their family's grocery. They see Breeze and give him a Black Power clenched fist salute as we curve right onto Hyde Street and start through the dips and rises of Russian Hill.

"I don't like your attitude, gripman," Jacob says from his permanent spot against the cabin wall.

"Mutual, Jake, I'm sure."

"It's 'sir' to you. There's no good reason you can give me for such abuse."

"How about you're too fat to stand in the doorway, Charlie?"

"No one speaks to me in that tone."

"Boy, what a wise guy. You really make conventioneers feel at home," the Greek chorus squeaks.

Breeze sticks his head out of the cabin and looks them over as slow as a big cat looking at prey. "You good old boys just about get the picture." None of them move as he goes back inside.

It gives me time to cool off. I'm holding steady on the grip handle and looking through the front windows as we drop over the edge of Hyde into a Number 2 hill, steep and long, the longest in the cable car system. The wharf is a miniature below, and the Golden Gate is disappearing into the Marine Hills far away.

No confrontation is worth it. Learned that a dozen times in my first year on the cars. But it never seems to take. Even if they're arrogant, nasty and stupid, they come for the city and the romance it always offers. They deserve the chance to find that.

"That was how you saw it, Teddy?" Superintendent Bailey leaned forward and looked straight at me, old man to son. The complaint was lying on the immaculate desk top like a bleached corpse at the edge of a dark pool. The office could have been vacant, because there was just one picture of his family, wife and seven kids on his desk, and the dust free walnut library table behind was empty except for some files and reports neatly stacked in the lower right hand corner.

"Yes, sir."

"About the 'fat Charlie'?"

"That too."

He picked up the city form. It was a single page with boxes to write in on both sides. "This is from Rabbi Jacob Goldski, United Jewish Reform Church, Dallas, Texas." He read through his bifocals. "As I boarded the cable car with my associates, a tall, blonde gripman, Badge #37295, turned to me and said, 'Move inside, Charlie, you're too fat to stand in the doorway.' That remained his demeanor during our entire ride to Fisherman's Wharf. I demand that some disciplinary action be taken against this employee to assure that other tourists will not have to suffer similar abuses."

Bailey raised his thick red eyebrows and sailed it back on the desk. "I see your point. But we have to remember, civil service is civil service." He looked out the high windows on the east wall, got up and walked around the desk. "Some guys you and me know around here would get a couple days off without pay for this. No questions asked." He picked up the complaint. "You and Breeze. You're good men. Dependable. You've got the best first year safety record for a gripman that I ever saw. I know everybody here, you know that?" Ted nodded. "Let me think on this one. We'll talk sometime tomorrow, okay?"

Ted turned and walked to the door. "You know, I apologized at the end of the line. Said I was sorry because it didn't matter who was right. I didn't want them to have a bad feeling about the city because of it."

He shook the report in his hand. "You apologized? What'd he say?"

"He just grunted and got off."

"*You apologized.*" He gazed at the white soundproof tiles on the ceiling. "You apologized." His big freckled hands tore the complaint into four neat pieces and dropped them into his empty waste basket. Chuck Bailey shook his head slowly as he looked across the room at Ted and smiled. "Some of these bastards want an arm and a leg."

The Cold War Burial

They had crossed the Sea of Japan and the plane, crowded with military personnel like him, was descending. Kempo Air Base, Korea. The time zones had kept changing and Ted's numbness had increased with each one.

When the first plane lifted off from San Francisco Airport thirty-six hours before, he knew Jenny was down there somewhere alone and waving, frightened. He'd felt it the last time they'd embraced. He couldn't see her. He couldn't look down and see her. And because of the angle of the takeoff, there had been no view of the city or Marin County, the coastline; just the sunset straight ahead and the sea growing rapidly darker to the horizon.

What time was it at home? Then make it up. It's five o'clock on, say, oh say, Tuesday or Thursday and Jenny has just completed another three hour session in her final studio class. She has put away her paints and canvas and is driving home to her parents out off Fulton Street by the park. Back in her own room after a year of marriage. Less expensive. They're nice people. In seven months it'll be May and she'll graduate. BA in Fine Arts. She's very good. What's the date today? Feels like winter. October. 5 a.m. Sixty-seven now, then back stateside in sixty-eight, November. Out by May or June of sixty-nine. Five months over already.

Ted looked down. In the first light there were praying mantis green Quonset huts and hangers scattered in the landscape mist and what looked like a black river to the south and east as the plane circled for its final approach.

His duffle bag was thrown in a pile with others on the tarmac. Everyone was staggering under the weight of the bags toward a camouflaged patterned bus a quarter mile away. He staggered with them. When they reached the bus, a sergeant started shouting out names.

There had been three months of basic training at Ft. Ord and two months of administrative and intelligence training back east in D.C.; he was nothing more than a glorified secretary really. They'd given him two weeks at home before shipping out. He and Jenny in her old room at her parent's. Two days in Carmel alone was all. When they let him out of here he'd have about ten months left. He wouldn't be going to Vietnam. Maybe they'd even let him out a little early. Four brokerage firms said they'd definitely consider him, and he could time his law school applications for September of sixty-nine. Pencil push the months away but no combat; the five days on the rifle range was all he wanted to see of that part of the war.

There wasn't going to be a sunrise, just the dimness receding as he stood dumbly and waited as names and curses spewed from the sergeant's foggy breath. The land stretched away flat and bleak to the south and west from the air field. To the north and east he thought there were low hills and raw, barren mountains beyond. He waited, gloved hands in the fatigue jacket's pockets, the flaps of the soft green baseball-like hat half covering his ears. He felt like a reluctant refugee. The bus pulled away, leaving a few civilians, some Marines and himself. A noisy C-124 cargo plane like he'd come in on took off a hundred yards away and disappeared into the white cloud cover, the engine suddenly muffled as if it had entered another dimension.

Far down the runway a polished, dark green four door military sedan came through the haze like an insect across the flat edge of a dying leaf. It stopped next to him. "You Ted Lawrence?" The driver was black. After the sergeant's, his voice was soft, almost like a child's. He wore the stripes of a corporal and a hat like Ted's, but the flaps were tucked under and there was a small silver O peace symbol pinned to one side.

"Lawrence, Ted. Private."

"I can see that, man. I'm from HQ."

Ted picked up the handle of his duffel bag. "You get to wear those things?"

He nodded toward the insignia.

"The Colonel, our dufus C.O., doesn't like it but what can he say? Our cats in 'Nam got 'em drilled into and painted on their helmets now. Throw your stuff in the back seat, but don't bury them two M-16s."

Ted placed the unloaded rifles carefully on the floor. "I thought we were administrative, paper soldiers? No guns, you know?" Ted climbed in next to him.

The corporal grunted with a grin as he swung the wheel and the sedan went into a long circular turn around the Quonset terminal and back up the side of the tarmac. It climbed a two lane road with new asphalt to the top of the dike separating the low lands on the airport side from the Huan River.

"George Melvin," he gave Ted a Black Power handshake. They drove along the top of the dike which was the MSR, the main supply route to Seoul. It was riddled with pot

129

holes. Melvin laughed, his left hand sweeping out the window in the chilly air toward the broad river and its muddy, half frozen banks. "Home away from home, mah man. Eleven months. The weapons? More Army bullshit. There's a good sixty miles of hard road to the DMZ, but these military fools figure, well, you and me, we're all of a sudden gonna get ourselves ambushed by a platoon walkin' down here from the North 'cause they ain't got nothin' better to do."

Ted took the offered cigarette and lit both of theirs. He was accustomed to smoking now after five months. Jenny didn't like it. "How much time you have left?"

"Twenty-seven days and I'm gone from here and out. Bye, bye Uncle. Back to the land of the big PX."

"Where are you from?"

"West Philly. Philadelphia."

"Never been there." Ted opened his window half an inch to knock off the ash. A little blew back in his face and he brushed it away.

"It's home. But you don't wanta go there."

"What are you going to do?"

"I got drafted, same as you. Was thinkin' about reenlistin' since I got me these corporal stripes already. I don't know. Sure as hell, they send my black ass to 'Nam. Shit, half my high school class went there. They even shipped some guys outa HQ here a month or two ago. Shortage of bodies or somethin' I guess. Maybe West Philly is better." Melvin laughed and smoke came through his teeth. "These regular

Armies are denser than a row a corn cobs in the sun. And even more paranoid. Last week, some North Gooks accidentally drifted over into the DMZ and us, 60 miles away, get put on alert by that dumb white boy colonel we got." He paused to inch around a barefooted old man pulling a cart full of anemic looking vegetables. "Next thing he'll do is try an Evac. Already threatened us with one."

"What's that?"

"Case they didn't tell you, this here is a mobile unit. Means in twenty-four hours or so we're supposed to load up and be down the road."

"Why would he want to try that?"

"He's a lifer, man. Got nothin' else better to do, and he might just score some points down in Seoul at the Big HQ or back in D.C. if it came off okay, which it won't, trust me. So, just accept it, we have to put up with their shit. No choice. Caught. I can tell you though, as fucked up as this operation is it's gonna be fun to watch, if it happens."

They drove slowly south in the early fog that hung close above the river, obscuring all but the road ahead. Besides the ancient jeeps painted red and yellow and converted into ever jammed taxi-buses, there were few vehicles except carts and bikes out that early. Ted kept watching the road creep towards them from out of the fog.

"You got a friend at HQ already?"

"Mike Larsen. Called him 'Big Skinny' since Basic. We've gone through all the same training together."

"Big Skinny," Melvin smiled. "Man, that's the perfect name for the cat. Must go six-six. A tooth pick." They passed a section of the river that was very broad and looked shallow. The banks there were well above the water's course.

"Why so many people down there this early? Fishing?"

Melvin steered straight armed, Grand Prix style. He wore a silver ring with the same peace symbol on his left middle finger. "Man, what kinda fish would live in that mud?" He thought about his question a minute. "Yeah, sometimes *tryin'* to fish. A few that got the bread for guns are shootin' ducks. Rest are buryin'."

Between the fog and the brown mud, it was hard to tell what they were doing.

"Garbage and junk?"

"Garbage goes in their gardens if they got 'em. No such thing as junk here. People gets buried down there. 'Course if the rains get heavy they'll be floatin' on down to Seoul." Melvin let the sedan drift right on its own like an old horse turning home, and it left the MSR and headed down a road of gravel and dirt and into the village of Yong Dong Po, next to HQ.

"Welcome to Gook City, mah man. The perfect place to spend a year with summer bugs big as your thumb," Melvin chuckled.

At a snail's pace, the sedan weeded its way among carts and bikes, people and motor scooters, passed stucco and wood storefronts whose wares spilled forth onto the imaginary curb. It must have rained in the night, because the streets were muddy and full of small lakes like the river. They were ignored except

132

for the frail kids who ran along calling out for candy, cigarettes and pennies. "This here's the Black Market capital of Korea. You got the bread, you can get anything from a TV to a jet fighter here. But smokes are the big item."

"They must sell the jets in parts."

Melvin smiled. "Nothin' would surprise me. Probably buy a woman here too." He swung right, onto a lane that was asphalt. Less than a quarter mile ahead Ted saw the gate and the double fifteen foot barbed wire fences of the HQ. "Beautiful, huh?"

"Fantastic. Just what I dreamed for."

"And only miles from the baddist of the bad cats. Gooks from the North coiled on a spring and ready to launch," Melvin kidded. "But with the roads bein' what they are we'd be long gone, unless we didn't know they were comin'."

Ted lit another cigarette as they waited for the MP to open the gate which, like the fence, was topped with concertina wire. Jefferson honked and waved as they drove in. The sedan stopped at the curb in front of the HQ main office. "'Fore you get out, it's time for my two-bit guided tour. On the left you got the colonel's private hootch and what we call our parade ground. Never seen a parade though. Those ugly Quonsets down there hold the PX, barbershop, library and snack bar. That's the BOQ beyond, and the Operations there on the left backed up to the dike. His hand shifted to the right side of the street. He was gesturing with the fingers that held a cigarette. They poked the air as if it were a balloon. "Over here is HQ, the club with good cheap booze and mostly ugly village ladies. That's the Mess Hall and the rest is barracks with the showers and shitters over there in back by the fence. Finally, you can't see it from here, comes the motor pool and that white building at the dead end next to Operations that looks like a church is, in military talk, our chapel, complete with a pasty faced white boy who sermons to any souls, especially Christians, that might be up that time of day, today, Sunday." He gave Ted another double grip handshake. Ted got his duffel out. "See you 'round, man."

"Thanks, George." The sedan pulled away slowly, quietly.

It was a little past six and the camp's streets were deserted except for the sedan which, trailing a plume of exhaust like clouds, cruised slowly down the company street and turned right, disappearing between the barracks and the chapel. A light breeze caused the ropes to softly tap against the empty flag pole over in the parade area. Even though the village surrounded the compound, except where it backed against the dike, the familiar drone of traffic so common back home was missing.

Reluctantly he picked up the duffel and headed up the gravel path. The first hint of cold sunlight hit the guard tower far down the fence. A Republic of Korea soldier, dressed like an MP, smoked and gazed off toward the river. Below him, just beyond the fence, a woman slid back the door of a house and threw something hot and watery from a clay bowl into the yard. Ted looked back at the HQ door. There was nowhere else to go.

It took only a few minutes to be processed, and he was again on the company's main street, walking towards his assigned barracks. The door opened before he got there. Mike Larsen, dressed like college in shirt, sweater and Levis, gave him the once over and frowned, but it instantly turned to a big smile and they shook hands warmly. "Enjoy the trip, Ted?"

"Oh, yeah, great fun. One hour of flying time for every four on the ground waiting. Three different planes."

"Me too. Wonder if anything works in this man's Army?"

Ted nodded. "So, what's it like?"

"About like the plane ride." Mike looked around as if taking in the whole country. "But we'll survive. On some levels at least." They both laughed. "I'll introduce you to the guys in our Quonset section and over beer and breakfast we can talk about when we're going home."

The Quonset, like a gutted and dried caterpillar, with its rounded, rippling green metal surface, wasn't half bad inside. It was divided into three sections, each with four identical bunks, foot and wall lockers, and an oil drum converted into a pot belly oil burning stove in the center aisle. Besides Mike, Ted's bunkmates were a lifer from Arkansas, a Sgt. Robbie, and another draftee, Doug, who had the ceiling and slanted walls in his area plastered with fold out magazine nudes whose leering, come-hither smiles were always there if you happened to look that way.

"Just throw your stuff on the bed. Moon'll put it away. Much better than you would."

The house boy beamed from a stool in the corner where he polished some combat boots. He wore rubber thongs, a rainbow colored Hawaiian shirt and G.I. khakis. "Welcome, Ted-san," He waved and went right back to the shoes.

Ted was glad to be back outside in the cold air. Jet lag was setting in. Across the company street the colonel, in a green

135

cotton bathrobe and pajamas, was hoisting the American and Company flags, and stopped to return their salute. His features were blunt, compact, under some brown hair that was parted way down on one side and combed across the top like kelp sprawled on a flat rock at low tide.

It was seven now and the club had just opened. Mike pulled back the green metal door and Ted almost stumbled in the deep red glow of the overhead lighting which mingled with hanging rows of bright yellow and blue Chinese paper lanterns. The cement floor and tin walls were painted purple. There was a small stage in the rear by the bar, and the dance floor was fringed with metal chairs and tables covered by blue cloths and empty wine bottles that each held an unlit orange candle. They moved tentatively in the red darkness to a table near the long bar. A girl who Ted figured couldn't be more than fifteen came silently through double swinging doors next to the stage. She was very small boned with an oval face and her skin was like smooth dried mud. The girl smiled, looking into the space between their heads at the wall. They ordered San Miguels with steak and eggs. She went behind the bar first and came back with the beers and chilled glasses.

"Beer of choice, Ted." They toasted.

"Tell me what else we worry about except lunatics bent on our demise from the North."

"On both sides, that's the biggie." Mike's Zippo flame engulfed the end of a Camel and he inhaled quickly. "I've been here eight days now and still can't shake that."

"You mean, 'why us'?"

Mike gazed at his long thin fingers. "All of it. Feeling utterly lost, helpless, meaningless, combined with the crazy, irrational sense that they're going to attack, while you and I are here. Melvin tell you about the evac shit?"

"Yeah."

"Guess the biggest concern is getting shipped to one of the outposts. Or even "Nam." Mike put out his cigarette and lit another. "While I was waiting for my operations clearance, they had me ride shotgun with a courier to the 306th outside Taejon down south. This is easy." His thumb nail tapped the beer bottle. "That is pure crap. Like regular Army. No house boys, no civies, regular inspections and all the rest of the B.S. we were so overjoyed with in the states. The whole moron thing."

The girl served them, smiling at the plates which seemed too burdensome for her small delicate wrists and hands. Mike watched her legs as she walked away. "That's strictly off limits. Even a movie." Ted nodded as if he'd assumed as much and wouldn't have anyway. "Her father runs the club. Sgt. Robbie told me a guy tried once a couple years ago and ended up in an alley."

"A couple of years?"

"They'll play the little gook who waits on nice American G.I. just so far. Yeah, Robbie's been here three years. Got a hootch and a mama-san in the village. Says he's extending until they throw him out. Beats stateside duty all to hell."

"Anything else to share."

"The milk tastes like somebody pissed in a bucket of chalk and then added water. But the food isn't bad. Head cook makes deals with a buddy at the General's Mess in Seoul. Two cases of prime scotch a month and we eat filet once a week that was meant for them."

Ted sipped his beer. With some A-1 sauce added, the steak tasted good. A tall soldier with a blonde butch and dressed in a black suit, tie, shoes and a white shirt, came in with a woman about fifteen years older than him. She was made up to look his age and wore the Korean version of a kimono whose colors matched the hanging lanterns.

"That's Sgt. Wilson from some place in middle America. He always had religion and now he's got him a mama-san too. Sunday breakfast, then listen to Captain Pasty at chapel. The good life, right? Wilson's one of the base's biggest Regular Army assholes."

"We'll be able to write the history of sarcasm by the time we leave." Mike laughed but said nothing. Ted couldn't believe he was thinking about a naked fifteen year old girl with light mud colored skin.

"Sarcasm? It's the Mama's milk of our survival, my friend, assuming the evac or a bunch of deranged Orientals from the North don't do us in first." Mike pushed away from the table. "I'll give you the five minute tour of the compound and then we'll walk to the village before your time lag puts you down for a nap."

The compound actually took less than five minutes. The library had only a dozen shelves, filled with western paperbacks and old newspapers and magazines, except for a ragged 1950 Encyclopedia set. The PX was mostly hygiene and candy and the snack bar served soft drinks, malts, bags of potato chips, fries and hamburgers, plain or cheese. "That's about it. Let's talk a stroll into the village."

They stopped to change into uniforms, no civies allowed off HQ. By the time they'd returned to the company street the base was slowly coming alive with other green clad figures moving from building to building in the random rhythm of small tropical fish beneath the mist of an ascending orange sun. The big gate was closed. They had to exit through the maze-like personnel gate which was caged in from above. There were about two dozen Koreans dressed in suits and western dresses standing patiently and silent outside. "Mother's milk of the chaplain," Mike said out the side of his mouth. "The born again. Or maybe it's the first time, seeing they've never been Christians before."

Yong Dong Po came up around them at the end of the asphalt lane. Ted felt the itch of his new woolen uniform, but shivered; the mist seemed colder, more penetrating as the sun rose. "You get the impression this place is dirty? Not the people, but…." His voice trailed off as he pointed to the wall next to the shop entrance which was covered with hand prints and the splatter of carts and other vehicles.

"Cold mud in winter, hot in summer, is how Sgt. Robbie describes it."

They stepped up into the archway of a porch to avoid an ox pulling a "honey" bucket. A shovel dripping with animal and human excrement dangled and clanged against the back of the cart as it plowed through the mud.

They'd just reached the heart of the village when Ted turned back. "Jet lag." They returned to the camp in silence.

Outside the gate, they used brushes and a hose to clean their boots. Ted finished and stretched, his hands spreading toward the yellow light in the mist. "Why us?"

Mike laughed. "Maybe spending time in hell makes everything else all downhill."

"One less mistake."

"Who knows, we might find a girlfriend who'll make us spicy meat, vegetables and rice. Rub our back with porcelain fingers."

Ted slept the rest of the day. When he awoke, the mist was turning gray outside. After chow, they spent more time at the club, and he fell early into a pleasantly drunken sleep.

He didn't know how long he'd slept when the night was shattered by someone in full combat gear shaking him violently. "Hit the deck, troop. Red alert!"

Mike and Doug simultaneously shouted from their bunks, "Get the fuck outa here, Wilson, you lifer moron! We're not buying any."

Ted's body shook with the adrenaline rush as his eyes groped in the darkness for something on which to focus. By the red glow of the stove, Wilson was standing precariously unsteady. His rifle was resting on the floor like a cane to prevent him from falling forward with the weight of the full field pack high on his shoulders, and his helmet was cocked awkwardly to the left, blocking his eye. "Captain Martin's orders." He was almost hyperventilating. "Full combat gear and down to Operations in five minutes. Otherwise," he paused, trying to

140

decide what the alternative was, "well, ah, you could get court marshaled!"

The door to the front section of the Quonset banged open and someone shouted, "Blow it out your rosy red, you ass kissing son of a bitch!"

Sgt. Wilson started to lurch in that direction, hitting the closing door and banging it open again. "This is a real evacuation. The North Koreans are attacking!" His boot tripped on the doorsill and he was propelled by his own momentum miraculously past the stove in the front section, crashing against the outside door and falling into the darkness as it swung open. As the door closed, it sounded as if he hit the cement path hard, but nobody bothered to look.

The guys from the other two sections drifted in wrapped in green wool blankets, and the lights went on, naked and bright. Nobody spoke. They stood uncertainly for a moment like old men in an airport. Outside, Wilson had recovered and was running from barracks to barracks shouting. A guy from the front section broke the silence. "Shit." Slowly they began getting their gear together.

Combat ready a half hour later, Ted and Mike walked down the company street, joining others who were filing out of the barracks. Above the Operations building the first hints of purple and orange light outlined the figures and carts on the main supply route above as they moved toward Seoul.

"They don't look too concerned," Ted said.

"This is all just more crap." Mike lit a cigarette and belched out the smoke. "I think"

The road in front of Operations and the chapel was already choked with trucks, jeeps and sedans. Somebody shouted directions hoarsely over the Company PA system and the words sounded jumbled, disjointed and slightly mad.

So many people were flailing about directionless in the Operations area that for the next thirteen hours Ted and Mike shuffled in and out of their department offices trying to look busy but accomplishing nothing. Files would get loaded onto trucks only to be recalled with curses. The shouting never stopped, and every chance they got they'd linger outside to watch Wilson, his uniform now drenched with sweat even in the twenty-five degree weather, arms waving like a man falling from a high cliff in full combat gear as he tried to direct but mostly was ensnarled in the mess of vehicles gridlocked all round him.

No one really knew when the Evac finally ended, but sometime just after six, the PA garble turned into a trumpet playing "Call to the Colors," and without a curse or command everyone stopped what they were doing and filed out onto the company street and waited in clumps wherever there was any space between the vehicles and equipment while the arch lights in the guard towers played with the shadows around them.

The colonel stood in front of the chapel next to the chaplain and raised his hand as if to bless them. "We see what has to be done. We see how far we have yet to go. We will continue to prepare because we will not be unprepared and allow the Communists to swoop down from the North." He came crisply to attention, clicking the heels of his knee length English riding boots together. Clumsily, everyone did the same as he motioned to the chaplain who took one step forward, thrusting the Bible he always carried towards the winter night's dull and chilling darkness.

142

His voice was too small for the moment and seemed to disintegrate like mist from his breath rising off bluish lips. "Remember, men, the Evac of the Israelites across the Red Sea. Remember and be of good faith." Twice he pushed the Bible heavenward.

"We learn. We never retreat," the colonel cried out. "Mess call will be at twenty-hundred hours. I think we can have everything back in order by then. But remember what we've learned." He paused and looked slowly around. The chaplain still held his Bible high. "There will be another Evac! Dismissed!"

But it was almost twenty-two hundred hours before the company street was neat and bare. The shower building was too crowded to try, and the mess hall food cold. Mike and Ted had chili burgers and whiskey at the club as they watched the village whores beginning to drift in alone or with a G.I. boyfriend.

After eating, they decided to try the showers again before the floor show. They stood under the soothing warmth until the next in line demanded a turn. Back in the Quonset they toweled off practically on top of the stove and then got dressed. Mike had on his college outfit and Ted, for no reason he could figure, was just putting on a clean uniform when Sgt. Robbie opened their door with his back and stood grinning like a short, dusty dwarf. "Gawd damn, it was colder'n a well digger's ass at the river." He held a shot gun and a green Army ammo box in one hand and two dead ducks in the other. He dropped the ducks in the aisle at the foot of his bunk.

"How the heck did you get off post?" Doug asked.

"Never was on. Walked off last night to the hootch just like always. What happened?"

"We just had an Evac."

"Well, Gawd damn." Robbie laughed like a small boy with a mouth full of bubble gum, his cheeks expanding and contracting, mouth like a bellows with a clogged orifice. "Gawd damn." He sat down on his bunk. "Same old traffic jam?" They nodded. "Had one just after I got here. Same thing, just different CO." Unsnapping his fatigue jacket he pulled out a brown sack and handed Ted a bottle of Bushmill Irish whiskey. "My standard welcome, Ted." He pushed away Ted's thanks as he undressed. "Jesus, was it cold down there. Been out since three this morning."

Ted opened the whiskey and took a long drink.

"Not a bad haul. Mama-san will dress 'em and you boys can come over for chow tomorrow." He tugged at his boots. "Gawd damn, this winter's hardly started and already killing 'em off. Had to watch where we were shootin' there was so many." He looked at the stove and took a gulp from Ted's bottle. "Comin' up about an hour ago in the dark, maybe a sliver a moon. A young guy watchin'. Cryin'. You don't see that a lot. A little wooden box, like those small crates they ship ammo in."

"His baby?" Mike asked quietly through his cigarette smoke.

Robbie nodded, heading for the shower. When he returned, he, Doug and Mike went back to the club, but Ted remained lying on his bunk with his boots on. The entire metal surface of the stove glowed red in the dark. The Quonset was empty. Nothing stirred. He sipped the whiskey from the bottle.

144

At one point, he tried hard to hear some sound; all he wanted was a shuffle of sandals toward the shower building, maybe a muffled laugh from one of the Quonsets, the cry of a baby or even an argument from a hut beyond the barbed wire.

Whether he passed out or fell asleep, he wasn't sure. But it was three-thirty when he looked at his watch. Everyone was asleep, and by the stove light he saw that the bottle was three quarters empty. He got up from the bunk and braced himself against the wall locker. The two ducks were still there across the aisle on the cement in a small pool of blood. Grabbing his coat, he went out, only stopping at the front gate to show his pass before disappearing into the black and quiet village.

Ted hardly noticed the shops. The houses were just a blur, and the watery pot holes he stepped in now and then went unnoticed as his pace went from a fast walk to a run, onward up the road to the dike and down the empty MSR until he reached a foot path on the other side which led down to where he'd see the burials. Only then did he stop. The sweat beaded around his forehead at the edge of his fatigue hat and down along his cheeks and neck.

His steps were tentative, almost delicate, as he ascended the bank until the path ended just above the river. The morning breezes were quiet there. He squatted. For a long time he watched the river and the new light expanding timidly in the east until his breathing slowed to match the silent flow of the dark icy water.

Ted smiled as the day dream he'd carried since childhood approached. He was riding his bike home from school. He was, maybe, ten. Not the house where he grew up but one he wanted to be his. It was all stone and sloping roofs, fireplaces and high, broad leaded windows: English Tudor set well back from the street on a large rolling lawn, always green and dotted with oaks. From the windows of the second floor landing you could see the spans of the Golden Gate Bridge distantly pressed against the sky. He could feel the cobble stones of the long driveway as his bike headed toward the garage with its basketball hoop over the center door. He passed the warm yellow light of the kitchen window and saw the smile of the mother he'd always hoped for. He waved back.

The river was still there. He heard the water's gentle brush against the bank. Ending without ending, artery of dark brown blood in the land. How often had he longed for that house and those inside to embrace him. Dreaming, dream dreams. Anything but what had been.

The ringing startled him. It was the curfew bell from the village. Ted noticed his hands. They were muddy. Somehow, he was on his knees and had been pushing them over and over against the hard soaked ground, like a cat's claws kneading a rug. Though still sweating slightly beneath the layers of green cloth, he was sober. Day's light was still vague on the horizon. East. Where Jenny was. School, park, friends. Music. Life. He couldn't figure what time it was for her at that moment.

He rose stiffly and started to walk up the path. Without knowing how he knew, he suddenly knew. And he also knew that the fear of it may someday overwhelm him. But in that moment it was still dull and far away. They were going to send him south. Vietnam. Just like Melvin had said, "No choice. Caught."

When he reached the MSR, he saw the cart coming towards him. It had been poorly fitted with tires about the size of a jeep's, and the man pulling it was dressed in a G.I. fatigue jacket like Ted's, but his pants were native, billowing yet tight in the calves and ankles. The wooden sandals made a rasping sound on the asphalt. It was hard to tell in that light if he was old or young. His arms were stretched out, pushing, grasping the handles of the cart. He bowed slightly from the shoulders in passing and Ted returned it. Ted looked out across the river. The purple tint had grown in the darkness above the barren mountains to the north. When he turned back to the road, the cart had disappeared.

Madame E, Parachuting In

There was a far off bell coming closer. His arm gently arched from the bed, touched the clock, and the city's silence was there again except for Larene's muted groan as she turned into him.

The floor of the flat above their daylight basement moaned and sighed. Eduardo knew that Ted had just rolled quietly off the futon, leaving his wife, Jenny, to sleep. Seconds passed. A door quietly closed. A toilet flushed and the pipes in the wall sounded momentarily like a small quick stream until Ted finished shaving and it was quiet again. The clock was at four-ten. Ted was meditating now, "trying to" Ted would have said, and Eduardo knew his own time in bed was soon finished.

In less than forty-five minutes Ted would be off to work on the cable cars, politely pushing his old BMW motorcycle to the corner and coasting down Castro Street to 19th where he always stopped for a sack of coffee, juice and sweet roll at Hanson's Café. Only then would the bike come alive. Eduardo knew they'd probably never see each other again. He also knew that if he stayed he would most certainly be drafted into combat. After all, his delicate, almost fragile features did look Mexican even though he was born in Spain twenty-two years ago, Eduardo Miguel Sabiques. Three years of college. Majoring in English Literature and Philosophy. But no longer deferred as a student, because the draft board had said the clerical errors—not Eduardo's fault—on his last application were too late to correct, especially with a war in progress.

Ted was a good friend whose military time had ended abruptly after a year. While on R & R, someone dropped "acid" in his whiskey in a Saigon bar and he'd flipped out. After a month in the hospital he came home to Jenny. She'd married him before the military as a college grad who was going into stocks or law. Now Ted worked as a gripman, driving a cable car. The marriage had been slowly unraveling ever since his return. Ted reminded Eduardo of some high school classmates who'd volunteered in 1966; only a few returned, and Eduardo sensed that a few of them hadn't, really.

Instead of combat, his father was coming for him in an hour, and later that day he'd land in Guatemala City. His uncle would take him back with the right papers as a citizen again of El Salvador where the family had immigrated before coming to America. He could live there and maybe teach at one of the universities, after he graduated. Larene wanted to join him. He could only hope.

Against his will, he prepared to rise. He wondered what Madame E would think if she knew his reason for leaving. But it was less difficult to accept his departure than believe that their short, stocky landlady, with a last name impossible to pronounce, had actually worked in the French Resistance through all of WWII. Thinking of that always made him smile, though most of the time lately he felt as if all his energy had been drained away.

Last Sunday she fulfilled a promise made almost two years ago: an invitation to the four of them to dine at the home of her employer, the Hamilton's, one of the wealthiest, oldest and most powerful families in the city. A noted French cook, she'd been with them twenty years. Even the governor couldn't entice her away with the offer of a state government pension. So her widowed life had been lived at the opposite corners of the city, Pacific Heights and Noe Valley's 24th Street.

149

The three-flat, apartment building was a major part of her retirement. She'd stopped renting the top floor some months ago, and it now overflowed with antiques she had bought with her from France and kept in storage for over twenty years. Every Monday on her one day off she came to clean the steps from basement to second floor and the sidewalk. Last week she'd given them bus numbers and the directions in careful, almost mysterious detail before telling them to arrive at four o'clock.

On the bus ride over it was painfully obvious to Eduardo and Larene that the argument Ted and Jenny had had earlier wasn't over; they hardly spoke. Eduardo had tried to help Larene make conversation, raising one topic after another that under other circumstances they'd have discussed excitedly for hours. He gave up. Larene looked at him, rested her hand on his, and they stared out the window as the bus came out of the Filmore District, topped the hill and descended into the bay side of Pacific Heights.

The broad street had begun to fill with afternoon winter shadows as they landed and stood somewhat hesitantly on the corner directly across and just up from their destination. It was a massive two story all red brick affair at the corner, almost barn like with a high, wide front porch. The downhill side was flush with the sidewalk.

Un-beckoned, the words "Sunday shadows" came to Eduardo, and he felt, for no reason, a sudden melancholy. He repeated it in a whisper none could hear, like a melody, over and over, as they went across and downward to the service entrance, a large, thick, redwood gate built in an arch directly in the wall. It was impossible to look inside. Madame E had been very specific; they must enter here.

Ted glanced furtively from one stately house to the next. "God forbid that anyone see commoners entering."

Unexpectedly, Jenny laughed as he bowed, motioning for her to do the honors and ring the bell marked "Service." Eduardo half smiled at Larene. They waited.

Soon there were footsteps, muffled and descending quickly a long flight of stairs that echoed as if in a tunnel. The latch rattled several times impatiently, then the gate, as if being frantically pushed against from inside. "Oh, why does the house man never do what I tell him?" Madame E questioned from her side in broken English despite so many years in the country.

Finally, with Ted and Eduardo pulling from outside, the gate began to scrape against the archway and suddenly popped free to reveal Madame E. "A dozen times I have told him, but," her shoulders heaved, "another good for nothing Mexican. Does just as he pleases, yet Mr. and Mrs. allow it. What can you expect? Oh, I'm sorry. It's so nice to see you." She poked her head out and also glanced up at the houses across the street. "Come in now, come right in," she motioned like a cop moving heavy traffic in rush hour.

It grew dark quickly as Ted closed and bolted the gate. "All secure." He saluted, but Madame E was already gasping and climbing the cobbled steps through the stone arch tunnel-like rear entrance whose walls of heavy, smooth and protruding stones as large as small boulders converged ever upward to a door that was set so deeply in the darkness of a landing that it wouldn't be seen until she kicked and it creaked slowly open as if someone controlled its movement from within.

151

They entered the pantry's yellow musty light. Ted saluted again, closing the wooden door and thick steel latch. "All secure."

Through the pantry they came to the kitchenette's deeper yellow light. Its high windows set in the north and west corner of the house encompassed the green edge of the Presidio, the Golden Gate Bridge and Marine Hills, the entire bay. The late winter sun would have filled the room and kitchen beyond with an eerie brilliance, but lace curtains, looking hand-made and brownish with age, covered the windows, filtering the light onto a cherry wood Shaker table where place mats and silver service were already set, as if someone was always expected or preparing to leave.

The curtains were wrinkled. Had they just been let down? Eduardo wondered. Four tall, white, thin candles burned next to a flower arrangement Madame E had picked from the garden terraces behind the house. Without the high windows and those running the length of the long kitchen, the room would have been cavernously dark. The cross beamed ceiling was low, designed from another century, and, Eduardo recalled, the room was sparse, devoid of modern gadgetry except for the commercial size stove, the ice box, an ancient gritty toaster, and a hand squeezer whose porcelain was stained by the orange patina of long use.

"Sit now, everyone. Dinner will be ready when I come back."

Jenny looked at Ted with an affectionate bleakness as he pulled out a brittle Shaker chair and helped her into it. Eduardo's furtive glance mocked suspicion. "Wow." Everyone nodded. "Why is she so jittery?"

152

Jenny put the blue linen napkin in her lap. She and Larene wore sweaters and skirts for the occasion while Ted and Eduardo had on, except for the color, identical cord jackets with leather patched elbows, turtleneck sweaters and slacks. "She said the family, I guess that's just the parents, are up at their ranch in Mendocino. Not due back until next weekend."

"Yeah, but she's acting like they'll pop in any second." Ted drummed his butter knife on the place mat. "Here she comes."

"Let's just enjoy it, huh?" Jenny slightly raised the curtain to take in the view.

"Please, Jenny dear, better not." The curtain rustled back as Madame E poured red wine dated 1908. It was French and looked like it had been forgotten in the cellar. She poured herself a glass and they toasted her and each other. "From Mr.'s collection. They seldom drink since their son, the oldest child, died, and the youngest daughter entered Buddhist monastery at Mt. Shasta. Just oldest daughter and her husband left, they run the family vineyard and wine business in St. Helena now. But Mr. still goes every day to his law offices downtown." She shook her head as if such diversity was foreign to her and difficult to comprehend.

"The wine is excellent," Larene exclaimed, studying the bottle in the candlelight.

"Going to waste in the cellar. I sometimes get a little bottle for myself," Madame E confessed, then smiled, her lips curling outward to reveal rows of crooked teeth. The four applauded. She blushed under her light olive skin and went back to the kitchen. Suddenly she stopped, listening with her head cocked toward the kitchen door and the house behind it.

"What?" Ted asked in a hushed voice as if there was something to fear out in the house where they hadn't ventured. She waved her hand and his voice was silent. Eduardo tried to recall a scene like that from a movie or stage play. Maybe it had been a Gorilla Theater performance in the park. He couldn't remember. It was something to do with the way she leaned forward, crouching at the knees, shoulders back and her head to one side. The bun of her dyed deep red hair resembled a small top hat. For no reason he momentarily felt his stomach tighten, but it vanished as she stood straight and glanced back at them.

"That gave me quite a fright. I thought it was Mr. and Mrs. home early."

Larene got up and followed her to the kitchen counter. "Do they do that often?"

"No. It was just foolish of me." Madame E stirred hollandaise sauce in a small, white pot on a front burner, then took a rack of golden lamb, a loaf of homemade French bread, asparagus and au gratin potatoes from the oven, setting them on the counter as Larene spread out the plates. "There are always very strange sounds though. Especially when I am alone. Sometimes it gives me such a fright when the wind pushes at the windows. You can hear the rafters in the attic groan right here, even downstairs in my rooms." She shuddered and laughed.

"Sounds scary," Larene acknowledged as she served the plates Madame E filled. It was every day kitchen ware, chipped in places but fired with a bright Mexican floral design.

154

"And," she licked a touch of sauce off her finger and pointed it at them, "their son's ghost is here."

"Ghost?" Eduardo asked as they all smiled.

"It is the truth. I don't know if he is here all the time. But, yes, he is here."

"Like a wanderer, coming and going?" Jenny raised her thick, dark eyebrows but Madame E ignored the skepticism.

"Yes. Every Sunday night Mr. and Mrs. have the Oriental, Mrs. Yung. She raises him at the dining room table. I've listened at that door."

"Did you hear anything?" Larene had served the last plate and sat down.

"No. But they do. They talk like he is at the table too." She pulled up a chair by the window and sat away from the table with her glass of wine Eduardo had just refilled from a second bottle. "He was almost thirty. Later I will show you his room."

And twice during the meal she stopped the conversation to listen. But it was just more sounds from the house beyond the kitchen. Although she didn't eat, telling them she seldom ate what she cooked for others, Madame E did take modest joy in their appreciation and appetite for the food and wine.

They'd nearly finished when Eduardo realized that, unlike so many other meals lately with Ted and Jenny, this had been one of laughter and light conversation, banter by which Madame E had revealed a dry wit that grew bolder the more pinkish her temples and forehead became. It was strange not to speak of ideas they cared about: Vietnam, civil and women's

155

rights, the death of the environment, the government and all the assorted myths of so-called democracy. Perhaps, Eduardo contemplated, it was the house that had either heard or never heard these debates and whose silence and distant sounds were a request that such talk was of no consequence here.

After Cherries Jubilee, they all pitched in to clean up. When they'd finished, Madame E, with quiet ceremony, withdrew from the refrigerator an unlabeled bottle of champagne and grinned naughtily. "Mr. has forgotten these too! The darkest part of his cellar. It is from a region just south of the Belgian border. Isolated. Pure. Virtually unknown and seldom shipped from the district. And never sold commercially in this country. Six generations have made it." She popped the cork. Only mist arose. The chilled glass of the flutes was as smooth as skin to the touch. There was a toast but no speeches. "Now, we tour," was all she said, opening the door to the dining room. They filed before her into the main house.

There was a muted sun that bought dusty light down through a series of three stained glass windows depicting the birth, death and resurrection of Jesus Christ, and it had settled on a fifteen foot long walnut table, pocked and peeling in places: a surface having long ago lost its luster, clouded like a delicate almost invisible algae or fungus on a pond where animals never came any more. The high carved chairs' embroidery, worn through now, complemented the Oriental rug running to the edge of the yellowing hardwood floor where it ended in the crossing under the archway to the main gallery.

"Living room?" Ted's question echoed out into the vastness and Madame E repeated, "the main gallery," as if he hadn't understood.

156

The vaulted twenty foot ceiling had the cross members of a ship's hull. They stood by the archway looking up like peasants in the narthex of an ancient cathedral. At the far end of the room were four more high stained glass windows, two on each side of a brick hearth and fireplace reaching to the ceiling and balanced by a massive carved redwood mantle that looked as dry as sand. The stained glass was assembled in the deepest tones of red, green and blue, a sequence of hunting scenes, brutal and pastoral, from the Middle Ages.

French doors encased in dark oak opened to the flagstone patio and terraced gardens on the left. The view was a panorama of the entire San Francisco Bay. The wall to the right had a balcony above it which lead to the upstairs rooms, and below its railing, the entire gallery wall held glass enclosed book cases filled to overflowing. Ted opened one and took out a leather bound volume. Its dust drifted up into the stained glass light.

Madame E's broken English followed the dust as she tried to explain the history of the gallery's massive tapestry that hung from its center beam. Commissioned in Persia by the family's first patriarch, it illustrated his life in overlapping scenes. He stood as a young man in English riding clothing and brown boots. One hand shielded his eyes from a relentless sun as he watched a procession of Americans and Chinese emerge from a mine shaft on the barren hill behind him. Their crude wooden wheeled hand carts overflowed with black ore. They moved past him, as if he were invisible, on a dirt path which led into the center of the tapestry where it became the cobble stoned street of a city crowded with people and horse drawn carts and carriages. He stood in front of a row of prominent granite buildings. The patriarch was elderly now, prosperously rotund

157

in his cravat, dovetailed coat, top hat and gray striped trousers. It appeared as if he owned all that he surveyed. But, from the tapestry, his life seemed to have only a beginning and an end.

No one was really listening though as they slowly circled and explored the room, passing its only furniture, two large chairs pushed together by the fireplace whose green leather was yellow and torn in places. No one spoke. Madame E's voice continued in the relaxed drone of the wine she'd drunk.

Eduardo remembered stopping in the center of the rug, like someone in the ebb of a red tide, to stare at the roughhewed cross in bas relief above the archway into the dining room. Larene touched his arm. "So strange," she whispered.

He put his arm around her. "History?"

Ted was still engrossed in the book. Its first edition date was eighty years past, a classic of illustrated fairy tales. He was squatting, back resting against a glass case. Jenny came over and knelt down beside him to look, leaning into him for balance. His smile was tentative, delicate. Her brown eyes fleetingly studied his face before looking down at the book whose pages he began to turn slowly.

Simultaneously, they realized that her voice had stopped and Madame E was motioning from the archway to the front entry hall. They followed her up the wide stairway whose oak railing and banisters were carved in the Baroque tradition, but so dense that it was impossible for Eduardo to decipher any meaning, any purpose behind the intertwined figures of people, gods, monsters, plants and animals that spiraled upwards above an Oriental runner whose colors had disintegrated into burgundy ash.

Jenny was pulling herself up hand over hand like a child along the banister railing. "If they're old, how do they manage these stairs every day?"

"They fly." Ted pressed his palms against her back as if supporting her effort.

Madame E had reached the second floor landing and stood puffing on her short legs. "Sometimes I find them asleep in the chairs by the fire, but, but usually they ride up the service elevator in the pantry. Wait." A strong breeze had come up off the bay and the house, though oak and brick, was creaking again. She patted her breast and sighed. "I am sorry, I cannot help thinking…"

"We can go now if you'd feel better," Eduardo offered.

"Oh, my no. It's all right. I seldom have guests and I know Mr. and Mrs. wouldn't mind, I don't think. Come. Drink more wine." She motioned to Ted who poured champagne from the bottle he carried. Madame E started down the hall.

While it was wide enough to drive a tank through, the ceiling seemed quite low. The molding was painted a tarnished gold and was peeling. It was divided into squares of about fifteen feet each. These had been hand painted in the Impressionistic style and featured scenes of people by the sea, at a race track and engaged in other activities of summer and fall. They were scenes recalling moments, joyous and care free. "More family history," Madame E commented without looking up. "But Mr. and Mrs. have never explained them."

They were some distance behind her as she approached the first door. Ted whispered, "We're American aviators parachuted from our exploding aircrafts into the French country side. It's 2 a.m. The underground is coming toward us from the cover of a forest." Wide eyed he looked ahead. "Any minute there may be a Nazi sighting." Everyone giggled.

Jenny blocked his path, looked up at him and suddenly saluted Nazi style. Ted tried to keep a serious pose, but couldn't as he returned the salute and grabbed her around the waist. They embraced with laughter.

"Come now, come," Madame E directed as she disappeared through the first door. The four, arms around each other's waists, quickly followed, Nazi goose stepping down the hall.

Madame E stopped them at the door. "This is Robert's room. The son. The pilot. In the reserve Air Force. We must not touch anything. Mr. and Mrs. would be very upset." She spoke as if they were about to cross an unknown territory in which she could not be responsible for their safety. She led the way.

It didn't look like the room of a thirty year old to Eduardo. Except for a couple framed posters, a war pin up in a one piece white swim suit and another of a customized '32 Ford three window coupe, the walls were bare. A model P-38 war plane covered with dust and cobwebs hung over a small oak desk cluttered with college books, a beer can filled with pencils and pens, and a deflated, autographed football whose wrinkled names were undistinguishable. The wood floor was partially covered by a brown tweed hook rug. A cat's claws had torn up much of the threading.

The late afternoon light drifted through a single large window, closed and locked, and fell inside the half open double closet doors. "Don't you get the feeling his clothes might open to another world if we touched them?" Jenny quietly asked Larene.

"God, yes." Larene withdrew her hand from the dim shaft of light. "Like Narnia through the wardrobe."

As they were leaving, Eduardo noticed a WWI German helmet sitting inside the book case next to the desk. It was creased in two places on the top and left side and the hole near the front looked like it could have been made by a bullet. Its flared out design and dusty green cast caused him to hesitantly extend his hand, which hovered over it like one would, testing a fire or some unknown and possibly dangerous source of heat. Were there, perhaps, memories still warm, alive in its cold metal? Had it been worn by a soldier killed by the father of the boy who once lived in that room? Part of a costume he'd worn on Halloween or in a college play? Then Eduardo remembered Madame E cocking her head to listen; Ted had said a terrible presence was about to surprise them from beyond the kitchen. That feeling would not leave Eduardo as they filed into the central hallway. What was that presence "out there?" Some fear too unspeakable? Was it in the house or just in that room? The father's war? The son's? Now? Sunday shadows?

"Was he killed in Korea, Madame E?" Ted asked as the group turned and passed through a double door archway and short hall with walk-in closets on both sides.

"No. He was called up too late for that war. It was over before he got to Hawaii. His little plane crashed near where he was stationed. Just an accident. No one could tell Mr. and Mrs. why. And they know many very powerful people."

"Were you really a member of the French Resistance Movement, Madame E?" Larene asked.

"Yes, I was a cell leader. There were twenty-five of us: children, women, old men. My husband was killed in Italy."

"What was it like?"

"We were, all the time, afraid."

The master suite's windows were also on the north and west walls and she stepped quickly over to those on the west by the side street and looked down and both ways. She saw them looking at her and shook her head and shoulders. "I am silly."

The north windows faced the bay and were identical to those in the main gallery. There was a long, wide chairless balcony and French doors. A brown plant stood in a white pot to one side. Larene tried the door, but Madame E motioned "no" with a little nod.

Ted came over and looked out. "Great view. What was that, a cactus?"

"It's too far gone to tell now." She shrugged and they joined Eduardo and Jenny who wandered a room so large that it dwarfed its furnishings.

Nearly the size of the main gallery and with the same twenty foot ceiling, there was nothing but two twin beds with matching cherry wood night stands. Each held a lamp whose tattered brownish white shades tilted permanently toward the beds. A single book was on each table. The spreads looked like silk, once very expensive, but so many cleanings had left their floral patterns faded and dull. Between the beds were two metal patio chaise lounges whose green pads were badly stained. These were tight against each other and created a bridge from bed to bed.

"Kelly and Kyndra sleep here," Madame E exclaimed, slightly embarrassed. "The Labrador dogs of Mr. and Mrs."

"Kind of makes it hard for Mr. and Mrs. to get together much doesn't it," Larene asked of no one in particular.

"Oh," Madame E's lips formed the word like a smoker blowing rings, "not at their age…" She smiled as if Larene should have known such a thing.

Jenny was standing next to Ted. "Maybe we need a dog. We'd go to the park more. Just out, you know?"

"She's right, Ted," Eduardo interjected, "and taking in some music too."

Larene raised her hand. "I'll watch the dog that night."

Eduardo put his arm around her shoulders. "Tickets for Grateful Dead and Quick Silver a week from next Saturday. You know we won't be able to go."

"Where does the dog fit with the music?" Ted asked. "It's just extra weight we don't need now." He looked at Jenny.

"Come on, T-Man, music," Jenny pleaded. "It'd be fun. I won't smoke anything funny and nobody'll bite us."

Madame E was at the door. Ted looked her way but Jenny blocked his and stared up into his eyes. "Okay," he sighed. "Music but no dog?"

"Hey, gang, he'll go." Jenny punched his shoulder affectionately. "Thanks, Ed." Eduardo pressed his palms together in the gesture of a Hindu blessing, and bowed slightly.

Madame E was already halfway down the hall calling back, "Come now." Then she vanished except for her rapid, heavy descending footfalls on the stairs.

She had the front door ajar before they reached the parquet entry. Against one wall there was a pecan wood bench carved with initials, hearts and hugs signs. It looked more like furniture from a bus depot or park, and she took their glasses and the bottle and set them there. A sudden gust pushed the door slowly open. Madame E blocked it with her foot, then looked quickly out. "I am glad you could come. Now I think it is time…"

"Thank you, Madame E," they chorused.

Eduardo took her hands in his. "Good-bye, Madame E. I'll miss you." Although she smiled, Eduardo knew the meaning of his words was lost; Madame E was already thinking about double-checking to assure that all remained as it had been.

She waved from the early darkness of the high porch until they crossed over and disappeared in the climb to the bus stop. "Looks like when night comes the neighbors don't matter anymore." Ted smiled.

The breeze was stronger, and they huddled together for warmth. Jenny looked over Ted's shoulder at the house behind them; it was made of steel with only the hint of life or lamp light filtering through the high tinted glass. Ted opened his corduroy coat and surrounded Jenny with it. She held the flaps over herself and pressed against him momentarily. No one knew

164

when the bus was coming as they stood quietly waiting in the last mellow silence of the wine.

Finally Eduardo spoke. "So bizarre. Always this rush of being discovered, ferreted out at any minute. And, really, by whom?"

"And no place to run," Ted agreed, visibly shuttering in the cold.

Eduardo's eyes moved to the clock. He had to get up.

The bus still hadn't arrived, and they'd alternated between standing close and dancing in place to keep warm. Eduardo now stood apart, collar up and hands deep in his coat pockets, staring off toward the lights of Berkeley. Ted walked over and a little awkwardly rested his hand on his shoulder.

"Shit," Eduardo muttered.

"I can't know your side of it, Ed." As Ted spoke his fingers lightly messaged the shoulder. "I know the other though."

"But at least you got to come back."

"To be what? As one of the nation's military crazies?" Eduardo shook his head and kept watching the lights in their carousel charade up and down the spans of the Golden Gate Bridge like waves eternally poised in the night. "So what do I do now? I look, ask, try to what? What am I coming back to now?"

"What do you want, Ted?"

"I can't find spirit or ambition anymore. I should have done what you're doing. Or prison. C.O. Some honorable act in the face of this insanity. I was always just a talker, I guess. No guts. Maybe there'd be meaning now if I had."

"You didn't do anything dishonorable."

"I know. But there was no honor to it either."

"I'll be branded more than a crazy when the Draft Board and FBI find out."

"You'll make a good life down there, man. Doing what you believe in. Honorable. It already is."

"I know I'm right. But it's supposed to be wrong. Sunday shadows, you know?"

Eduardo turned and they embraced. The girls came over and joined in, all rocking slowly back and forth until they heard the lonely diesel engine of the empty bus far below, grinding upward to their stop.

Soon it would begin, his father on the stairs in half an hour. Yet he didn't move. He whispered to the first light, "Sunday shadows." They were the subtle hues waning in the afternoon streets and parks of the city that turned inevitably into another work week, an evolution without end: WWII, Korea, Vietnam and hundreds before.

Eduardo let go of the shadows and strained to hear the laughter of Jenny and Ted in happier days. Memories of the joyous times he and Larene had known them filled the room, and he hung on to these like the boy he was, clinging to a rock in a dream whose surrounding landscape was dissolving.

Sunlight Comes to Noe Valley

Actually, the truth is just the opposite, because if there's sun to be found anywhere in San Francisco, Noe Valley's where it'll be. You can be under fog from the Financial District to the Richmond, Fisherman's Wharf to Nob Hill, but above Mt. Davidson and the Twin Peaks there'll be a blue patch of open sky from Market to the Mission District and, sometimes, stretching down Noe Valley's narrow corridor to the south of Market, all the way to the docks.

The quality of its crystal light is rare in a city more famous for the romance of fog and the cold rain you step out of into warm bakery and espresso smells and small marble tables at the end of an alley you've never walked before. The quality of such light at its best always comes in October when the sun gives the fog a rest.

You'll never be more than warmed though you'd sit for hours on any given day on a porch, stoop, fire escape or roof top of the ancient Victorians that stand on Noe Valley's cross hatched streets, like rows of Tibetan monasteries, distant and formless as mist from the city's center. The breeze shares an intuitive agreement with the light.

Luckily, this is an October story in 1969 about two young people very near the end of the Age of Hope. It's a kind of love story, minus what the songs always tell you. No, Ted wasn't marking the calendar off until year's end, although he sensed that besides his marriage, the year was bringing other endings as well. Jenny left in July, four days after he'd held her against him wrapped in the flaps of his down parka as they'd watched the fireworks on the bay from the deck of a Telegraph

Hill apartment. He'd helped her move into a house of steel and tinted glass with a view of the park a block below UC Medical Center and not far from his old place where Ashbury was cut off at the Park's Panhandle.

He'd lived there at the beginning of the Age of Hope, late in '63, better known historically as "the sixties." Ted thought of the time between then and the end of '64 as the time of "the quest" when drugs were used more to enhance, not avoid, the rhythm, power and message of the sunrise or the latest rock group. Then, people from fourteen to sixty were struggling to open, hoping and dreaming for a world in balance, one they could fully embrace. It was in the air. You could almost wear it. But in those short months of laughter, introspection and sharing, a cycle of decline began. It wasn't recorded, even noticed by most, but it continued through the end of the decade as the streets of the Haight District grew grimy with owl-eyed spare change kids, junkies, and the undercurrent of violence that, now and then, surfaced as murder and death by overdose. And with the early undercurrents began the first migration in late '64 and early '65. Dreams had frozen in blossom.

Unbeknownst to Ted, he was on the cutting edge, one of the first settlers who came to Noe Valley. No, this wasn't some vast panorama of mountains and rolling landscapes; there were plenty of people there already: a mixed bag of Blacks, Orientals, Mexicans, Anglos, gays and straights, a mostly blue collar neighborhood happy with itself. He still lived there in the same three-room flat on 24th Street. But now, as the decade was ending, the migration had become a time when people were actually leaving the city. Familiar faces were disappearing. Two weeks ago, the three girls from the laundry at 19th and Castro that did theirs at the same time as Ted, gave him a hug and said good-bye. They were returning home to the east coast to begin college. Even familiar faces back as far as '64 were disappearing from the street and the counter stools and booths of Hanson's Café.

It seemed to Ted that all the decade's bright dreams were slowly dying. But not for him. America may have been grinding back to what it always was, but his was still that quest, however feeble: praying, meditating, searching for a miracle while nothing changed. He kept working his new four to midnight run as a gripman on the cable cars and began a single course, *Intro to Oriental Philosophy*, at SF State instead of Berkeley where he'd graduated three years before.

Last year when he returned from the war and by some miracle got his old place back, the house three doors down had been rented. The aging gay couple who'd beautifully restored it had bought another run down Victorian directly across the street and were restoring it. The new renters were two couples and two single people, a man and woman. They were all from Cleveland. The married couple had a five-year-old boy named Red Cloud because his mother, Liz, was a quarter Lakota. Her husband, Josh, went to work in a week as a boat mechanic down at the St. Francis Yacht Club. Ken and Caroline, the unmarried couple, waited table at a five star restaurant in the Marina. Ted seldom saw them. Mark, the single man, after some months of depression and searching, had finally found a job as a *Marine Biologist I*, working at the Aquarium.

Finally, there was Erin. She worked in a kind of left over hippie yarn and dress shop in North Beach, creating her own designs. Her days off were Wednesdays and Thursdays which overlapped with Ted's Thursdays and Fridays. He'd gone from early back to a late cable car run because night was the time he missed Jenny most.

Each day the sun was out, Ted moved his study of Oriental Philosophy to the front steps. Red Cloud and his mom made sporadic appearances on the sidewalk, their yard behind the house barely big enough to hang wash. Liz would set him on the low wall that separated the sidewalk from the steps down to their garbage and storage area and work with him on a crayon drawing for an hour or more at a time. On her days off Erin joined them, sewing her original designs into fabrics of rich Middle Eastern patterns. The designs were full, with large sleeves, and gathered at the waist. The length varied from mini to floor. She wore her floor-length versions so Ted had no idea what her body looked like, but her face always appeared radiantly healthy. The hazel eyes were deep set and her face wasn't gaunt or round but a gentle mixture of both and covered with freckles. He assumed she was Scandinavian because her waist-length, light brown hair had a reddish cast.

When Jenny was still there they had all talked on occasion as they did with the other neighbors on the block. The unmarried couple had a Honda motorcycle about the age of Ted's BMW, and he'd walk over to trade mechanical tips whenever he saw them working on it. The relationship with the group had evolved slowly, naturally, comfortably, and he recalled later that it was mostly with him not Jenny as he sat on the low wall munching some fruit Liz or Erin had offered and watched Red Cloud tear up and down the steps from the basement to the high porch. It quietly amazed him that so many friends lived in such seeming harmony and had traveled together half way across the U.S. on this adventure. He had lost contact with all but one person from high school, and as a commuter

170

student on a campus as large as Berkeley he never was close to anyone.

During the time he'd worked early cable car runs, he'd come home, showered and taken a book to the front steps to wait for Jenny's return from classes at State and to catch the last of the late afternoon sun before it moved west and the street became shadows. Since returning from Vietnam, he'd tried to get back into reading. He'd always enjoyed it, but his anticipation and attention would lag, usually after ten pages. So, he'd pretend to read while he watched the rhythm of the neighborhood.

Before getting his job, Mark would return like clockwork around 3 p.m. from his daily job search or Erin would pass and say hello, going to or from work. Then one day about a month after Jenny left, Erin paused long enough that he could ask if she would like to sit for a minute. He was on the top step, and, as if she'd always done so, she settled on the bottom, offering him a freshly purchased nectarine from a sack.

That first conversation wasn't much. They ate the fruit, and she had told him how much better it was "or at least tastes," she'd laughed, than fruit from Cleveland. But after that they spoke more frequently, Ted walking over to look at her latest creation or she, pausing to sit or lean against one of the stone pillars of his front porch.

They knew nothing about each other's lives beyond 24th Street, and many early conversations had to do with city politics, the Castro District and its shops and characters just down the hill, and the war. As to the war, Erin did most of the talking since Ted told her that he had nothing worth telling. Now, he was no closer to it than Eduardo, his friend who'd lived in the basement flat and left the country to avoid the draft. Yet she could call up the names of several boys from high school and her two years at junior college, who had gone, come back, or never returned. A former boyfriend had been among the latter. In the warmth of the porch she spoke of their brief histories, where they'd lived, their families, what some wanted to do after the war, in a way that brought them as close as the people on the block. She made it seem as if somehow Ted needed to know and care about their lives.

Since Erin liked the lower step and he the upper, they seldom looked at each other. She seemed to stare up beyond the rows of old houses rising block after block to the south and east as if she was looking for a true outline of Mt. Davidson. Her eyes were hidden by the long hair brushing against her temples, but now and then he'd glimpse her lips, soft and thin, or the movement of her chin. Though there was nothing intimate that they shared, after a while Ted would often feel as if he was not with a person but with the restful voice of a narrator that created the comfort of being alone. When she turned to see his response to a specific remark, he actually enjoyed their reassuring eye contact.

Yet, their conversations had ended abruptly the day the entire group was out on the sidewalk and low wall drinking a beer while Ted loaded Jenny's stuff into a friend's truck and drove away. In the past three months, Erin had always been pleasant, smiling, greeting him but not stopping, as he tried to make sense of the text book he now held on his steps in the first week of October light. It was almost four, starting to get cold, and the street was approaching the early fall darkness. He sensed her before he saw her coming up the street.

"Hi."

"How's it going?" Erin stopped to adjust the large hemp shoulder bag she carried as a purse and place for fabric.

"Not bad. How about you?"

"I'm late helping Liz with dinner." She smiled and turned.

"Hey." She looked back. "Was it something I said? Bad breath?"

She laughed, letting the bag fall to the sidewalk, and shook her head. "I thought you might need time alone?"

"But that was July 8. This is October."

"I rang the bell last month, but you were out. You've been out a lot you know." She pointed to his BMW at the curb.

"That much? I guess so. Rode down to Big Sur, spent a few days, and up to Petaluma and Bolinas a few times."

"I even waved on several occasions but I don't think you noticed."

"I'm sorry. Maybe I've been pretty abstract." He smiled as she shouldered the bag. It overflowed with fabrics for her exotic designs. "I missed you stopping by."

"Well, there's tomorrow?"

"Good." He watched her turn and walk up the street.

After work that night he laid in bed awake for a long time, his thoughts, mostly of the past, flowed by chaotic and unchecked like a storm washed river filled with debris that had once been part of the lives of a town flooded ten miles upstream. He knew that most of his classmates were already doing something, putting it together, churning out a Niche in the world beyond the night.

There was a half-moon through the open windows where he slept on the futon, and he got up about four to follow its whiteness until it ended near the kitchen archway. He paused, undecided, then passed into the darkness where he sat wrapped in a quilt at the table by the windows with a half glass of wine and, as he'd done many nights in the past three months, stared at the dark windows of Franklin Hospital on the far hill where the moon's reflection had settled brightly against the glass, like the white keys of a piano.

It was only nine-thirty when she came from the house with the overflowing hemp bag. He'd just settled against one of the cement walls of the porch with cereal and coffee. The best sun would remain there for a while, but he moved to the other side, leaving a small canvas pillow where he'd been. "Morning. I didn't expect you until after lunch."

"I'm always awake early now." She climbed the steps and neatly laid out some fabric on the low cement wall behind her and on a sheet she spread on the porch. He thought it was the first time they'd sat on the same level.

"What's your tea flavor this morning?"

"You actually have tea?"

"That I do. Stopped last night before work at the shop you told me about in Chinatown."

"Thank you. Anything's fine."

"Green or Jasmine?"

"Jasmine."

He returned in a few minutes with the tea in a dark blue mug like his and a part of a pastry.

"Come on, it won't kill you," he joked, since she went light on sugars.

"Can't turn you down." She took a bite and a little tea. "Both excellent."

"Glad you can admit it."

"Just because I was raised on gravies and beef, not to mention desserts, doesn't mean I can't change." She took a second, very small bite. "But it's not always easy."

"I know. I was raised the same way. I just can't get into brown rice three times a day."

She smiled. "I hope I never do. But I've learned to love getting up early. That's a change. Five o'clock now, every day."

"Me too, even earlier when I had the early Hyde Street run."

"Back home I used to sleep until ten."

"But why do you get up early now?"

"To meditate. No one's up. In India they call the very early morning, say, three to six, 'God's hours'."

175

Ted had tried to meditate but always got so distracted, and Jenny thought it was weird. "My meditation is dropping down the big Hyde Street hill with no one on the cable car but me and my conductor at about five-fifteen on a day like today, totally clear, no haze even, and seeing the sun just coming out of the east, touching the bridge, lying against the hills over in Marin. I lived for it. It made the whole day, the first romance of the day, and it didn't matter what kind of tourist or traffic crap came later, the day was still going to be good."

"I'd hear you pushing the bike to the corner sometimes. You never start it."

"I coast down to Hanson's for a coffee and sweet roll. There's more traffic and noise that early down on 19th."

"I'd call that a one percent deed." Erin was working on the sleeve of a dress which was of a different fabric and pattern than the main body.

"I don't understand."

"One percent or less of the motorcycle riders, or people in general, would be that considerate. How come you changed over to night work? School?"

"That was part of it. I never have liked night much. It's boring, so I'd rather work days."

"Now that I'm up early I understand. My best time is from five or six to maybe lunch time. In the afternoons at the shop I'm kind of dazed out, but I do pick up some at sunset for a couple of hours. After that, in bed by nine. So, I have a rough time once in a while when the owner wants me to close at night. I just wish that our house and this street were a little more quiet."

"That last trip to Big Sur, I spent three nights in a cabin I heard about. It was nothing much, but there's a stove and refrigerator. It had a great fireplace, the only source of heat. The old guy who rents it has six or eight he's built over the years, and they're way apart so it's like being out there with no one. I didn't like it much the first night, but then it was great knowing the silence would be there the next morning." Ted held his cereal bowl to his mouth and drank the milk Oriental style. "Excuse my manners."

"Mind if I ask a personal question?" Erin had stopped sewing.

"If it's about Jenny, I haven't seen her since she moved out, except at court on the divorce and a couple times at school."

"I know it's been really rough for you. I could tell just watching you come and go."

"I've had my bad moments. I didn't want it to fail and become just one of the many. I guess she's practically a mother now."

"Pregnant?"

"No," he laughed. "The guy she's with, her drawing instructor at State, he's got two little ones living with him part of the time. I just saw them for a moment in their yard. They looked about second or third grade."

Erin picked out more fabric from her pile and gazed up at Mt. Davidson for a long time. "Remember the guy I said I dated who didn't come back from Vietnam? Truthfully, he wasn't killed or even drafted. He didn't want to be tied down so he kind of disappeared about six months..." she hesitated,

177

"...after we were married. Even his parents didn't know where he was."

"How come he wasn't drafted? Being married wasn't a sure thing."

"I was also pregnant when we married. He left a couple months before I gave birth." She looked up from her work with a small, strange smile. "She died. Too small, born too early." She never stopped sewing. Ted didn't know what to say or do, and his lips felt like they were caving in as he moved over and stopped her hands, holding them in an awkward way. She could see his eyes and reached out accepting his sympathy, rubbing his cheek and chin softly. To him, hers was the most affirming gesture he could remember, and as he settled back in his place he was so relaxed that he felt, for an instant, as if she had covered him with a presence of wellbeing or such a presence had covered both of them. "I was pretty much a mess for a while. You know, my family not being very supportive, and I was just barely out of high school. It was like being tolerated. So I had a crazy aunt. Or so my family thought. And she let me come live with her on the other side of Cleveland in this tiny house in a neighborhood this close," she measured for him with her thumb and index finger, "to becoming a ghetto." I commuted to the junior college and started helping her with the little tailoring business she ran at home after my uncle died. I liked it, as you can see, and took some design classes. End of story." This time her smile was warmer. "Hadn't you better do some studying?"

He brought the book out from his table and slid his back down the wall onto the pillow. She gave him a clownishly glum look. He nodded. "It's not my favorite pastime, but then, I haven't figured out what that is yet."

Erin held out her hand and he gave her the book. It was heavy, and she dropped it on the dress she was sewing and began fingering through it after reading the table of contents. "You know, Ted, I distrust books that give you giant ideas in chronological order."

He grinned and forced himself to open it. They worked in silence for over an hour. It felt so natural to be sitting there with her, as if it was exactly what they should be doing in that place and time. Finally, she asked if he thought it was about eleven.

He crawled over to the entry, stretched out and looked through his open door. "You must be one of those psychic time keepers."

"I am. Unfortunately, I have to go over to the store and meet a customer at noon. It's a custom design."

"Can I take you on the bike?"

"I'd like that sometime, but I have to take the dress too, which won't fit on the bike."

"Okay, maybe tomorrow?" Ted asked. She nodded and let him help carry her material and sewing gear back to the house.

But it was a week before they met again. On short notice, Ted had his first paper due and Erin got two custom orders that had to be done immediately. The following Wednesday, Ted was hurrying out to the campus library. She was on her porch talking to Liz, who Red Cloud was trying to pull down the stairs. Erin called out to him, "How are you?"

He put his notebook in the bike's leather saddle bag and walked over. "Okay. Finished the paper and have to go out to school and use one of the library's typewriters. Then it goes in."

"How'd it come out?" She walked down the stairs, the folds of her dress getting caught up in a strong, sudden gust out of the breeze that had begun at dawn.

"Not bad. It was actually interesting to research and instructive to write. The dress situation under control yet?"

"If I sew all day at the store today."

"What about taking a ride out to the park tomorrow? We could get sandwiches at Hanson's."

"Those are all so big and beefy. Will you gamble on vegetarian?" He smiled. "I promise it will be edible."

"I believe you. Can I bring some drinks?"

"Nothing."

"Thanks."

"Better wait and see." She gave him her glum look, smiled and climbed the stairs.

Ted spent part of the next morning cleaning and tuning the BMW, and was showered and leaning against it when she came down the stairs. He took the heavy hemp bag from her, feigning weakness, staggering to the bike as she laughed. He doubled the strap around his neck and set the bag on the gas tank.

"It'll be lighter, hopefully, after lunch," she predicted, climbing on behind him. "Do we have a destination?

"I was thinking about Sheep Meadow but that still gets crowded. There's a place I found all the way at the other end of the park. It's near the old windmill just off coast highway. It's through a fern forest and you can't hear much traffic."

"Sounds really good." Ted fired up the engine.

Everywhere you went, from the long shore docks to the beach end of Golden Gate Park, the city was touched by a variation of the light in Noe Valley. Her hair was blowing around his ears and cheeks. He didn't try to brush it away.

They reached the ocean side of the park and Ted navigated the BMW into the thick matting of leaves. They passed through the windmill's ever changing shadow as the wind shifted in the surrounding canopy of tall eucalyptus. The grey, weather-weary wood of the main tower had been torn off in places like its vanes, and the sails had long ago disintegrated. The engine was silent. They walked quietly through the giant ferns brushing their bodies and faces. As the path rose slightly the undergrowth increased until they were like two lost figures in an unmapped forest. The density lasted only a minute and they came out into a small clearing just elevated enough to see the startling light on the sea beyond. By October, most of the prairie grass was dying out and they laid down a blanket at the foot of a massive eucalyptus facing the water.

Erin neatly placed the lunch before them while Ted looked slowly around the clearing. The light seemed thicker, not murky but marine-like. No one had been there for a long time. She handed him a plate with some corn chips, a slice of dill pickle, a deviled egg and a sandwich on homemade whole wheat with tomato, avocado, sprouts, lettuce and a thin slice of Monterey Jack cheese. "Do you mind tea?"

He shook his head and took the cup from her. "Smells like peppermint. Tastes nice."

"It's totally Chinese. I can't even pronounce the herb, but it has a sweetness that's not over powering. Soothing to me."

"I agree. So, anything of interest happening over at the commune?"

She laughed. "That's what it feels like sometimes. I'm ready to try living like you. All's well except for Mark. His draft notice arrived from Cleveland and he's only been at the Aquarium three months."

"That's a disaster. After all the time he looked for a job and now finally finds the right one. What's he going to do?"

Erin paused to finish chewing some of her sandwich. She smiled secretively before speaking. "It'll take some weeks before he's reassigned out here and between now and then he's decided to progressively take larger doses of LSD."

"What good will that do? Don't you think that could be dangerous?"

"He figures if he gets really stoned just before reporting, then that's how he'll act at his draft physical and they'll give him some kind of psychological discharge. Lots of people did at home and some succeeded."

"Wouldn't it be safer just to leave the country? Eduardo, my friend who lived downstairs, did that last year. I hear more people are getting zapped on drugs lately."

"That girl in the *Chronicle* from Stanford up in North Beach who jumped off the Broadway tunnel?"

"Yes." Ted had finished his sandwich and was sipping some tea. The last steam rose. Gazing through it, the light in the clearing looked even more thick and weighted.

"What is it, Ted?" She was sitting with her legs straight out and had removed the burgundy Chinese shoes. He watched her feet and ankles; they had the same freckles as her face.. She wiggled her toes to get his attention.

"Ted?"

He looked up. "I'm pretty mainstream, I guess, Erin. From personal experience, drugs scare me. You're so out of control and no way for a time to regain it." He felt a chill and drank more tea.

"I'm convinced that it's either where your mind is at the time you take it, or where it secretly is all the time and you don't even know it. Acid can bring that out."

"What about that girl on the tunnel?"

"You're trying to tell me something, aren't you?" She touched his leg with her toes. "I can feel it." He nodded. "You can, you know. If you want."

"I know." He stood up and stretched. "Thank you for a wonderful lunch."

"Homemade chocolate chip cookies still to come." She lifted a plastic bag from the hemp purse.

"No sweets, huh?" She grinned. He kept on rotating his torso and stretching. "Section 8," he said after a long silence.

"What?"

"That's what Mark's looking for, a psycho discharge." Ted gracefully settled to the ground. "It's what I got." She was quiet, looking at him as she had when she touched his cheek. "I hated the military from the first day. Power in the hands of idiots. And the worst is a draftee, or anybody for that matter. Can't do a thing about it. You're trapped.

"I did get a little luck at first and wasn't trained for the infantry. Went to a so-called intelligence-clerical school and they sent me to Korea. But I was there only three weeks and got shipped to Vietnam via Okinawa. First they gave me a month's training in jungle tactics, not office work. They were short of men. There'd been a big kill off. What could you learn about survival and combat in that time? And to make it even worse they assigned me to this elite Marine reconnaissance team. It was nuts. I mostly carried maps, a radio, extra ammo and my rifle. They probably hated me because I wasn't one of them. Why shouldn't they? Hell, most had trained for months and here was some draftee punk on their team who didn't know jack shit. In their line of work they didn't need a screw up along."

"What were they supposed to do?"

"Try and gather information about the enemy and sometimes get shot or killed doing it. We were helicoptered to the Cambodian border in the north where Laos and Vietnam meet. Then we crossed over, looking for what was supposed to

184

be a supply route through Laos and down between Vietnam and Cambodia. Most of the guys loved it. It was a big macho adventure. We never found anything, but to me it was living twenty-four hours a day with almost more fear than you can stand, fear of being discovered, being captured and tortured, fear of finding Viet Cong, fear of being shot in the head in your sleep, if you could call it sleep.

"Once in nine months, we hiked back over the border and got R&R for seven days. On the way south, the chopper set down to pick up a couple guys at this Marine fire base, a camp in the middle of nowhere surrounded by barbed wire and probably Viet Cong too. They had this bamboo prisoner's cage they'd liberated from an enemy camp somewhere. It had bamboo bars on all sides and you had to kneel and half bend just to get inside.

"When they stumbled onto this camp, a village, they found four G.I.s in cages. They tortured and killed everybody from little kids to old women and rescued the prisoners. Only one survived the helicopter ride back to the fire base and they brought the one cage with them. The guys who had leveled the village were long gone, dead or stateside, but they kept this thing around like a shrine. I got up close to it and it looked like dried blood all over one side. Jesus. For some reason I could never figure, when I left the fire base my fear got even worse." He stood up abruptly and began stretching again. "How I got through it I don't know. I felt like it was all so stupid and meaningless on one hand and like a wimp and coward on the other.

"Anyway, we thought we were going home, but in Saigon for R&R we learned that we had to go back for another two months to complete our eleven. That, after being out there nine months straight. We had five days. The first night we went into town to get drunk. The guys I was with were mostly into hash and cocaine when they could get it. They were really okay guys, but from a different world than mine. Mostly really poor families and little education. I'd always refused drugs in the field, which only made me more of an outsider. They kept saying it would relax me, that's why they did it. But I was just so wound up with fear.

"So they decided, as a joke, to drop a half sugar cube of acid in my bourbon, and in a half hour I completely flipped out. All of a sudden the whole bar, Vietnamese and Americans, looked like my enemy and I thought they were out to get me, to put me in one of those cages. I felt like they were pushing me in, poking and stabbing at me through the slats. I guess I nearly tore the bar to shreds. Later, the doctors said I thrashed and fought so long and hard that I should have passed out. But I didn't stop until they sedated me and got me to the base hospital." He sat down again.

"The next day it had worn off but I was having lots of flash backs of being in the cage while Viet Cong, kids to elders, constantly poked or speared me with bamboo poles. I had no food, no water, no bathroom but my pants. I kept crying out for them to stop but they wouldn't. In a week I was fairly stable and they shipped me on a medical plane to Hawaii." He'd been staring at the sea the whole time he had talked and suddenly realized that Erin was on her knees in front of him, rubbing his hands with her fingers. The hazel eyes kept moving from his face to his hands and back. "Thank you." He raised her hands and held them against his face for a moment. Then he set them on her knees. "It's been over a year. I'm able to relive that scene consciously and I can handle it, except once in a while when it still comes as a nightmare, though it seems to get less terrifying even then. It's supposed to be that delayed stress syndrome.

"I was in a military hospital in Hawaii for a month to six weeks, I forget, and I snapped back pretty quickly, because I was off medication in two weeks and spent the rest of my time talking to a psychiatrist and body surfing. None of them could help me understand what it all meant, but I was fully functional and surprised they let me out. Even wanted me to continue therapy at a VA hospital, but I didn't.

"I made Jenny promise never to tell our parents the reason I got out early. Of course, it was a complete shock to her. I'd gone in this college guy she'd married who was planning on going into investments or law, maybe an MBA. Instead I came back and started working on the cable car, which has helped for reasons I don't understand except it's taught me something about the basic dignity and strength of people, regardless of their politics or background. Guys I work with do incredible kind deeds every day and nobody knows it." He glanced at the cookies. "That's it. Like you said, end of story. How about a cookie now?" They laughed together.

"No one ever described it to me like that, Ted. The boys I knew were never big on conversation anyway, but they didn't speak much about the war. I can't even imagine. That constant, piercing fear every moment. Like being pushed into a big room with dozens of doors in each wall and told by people who you know don't care about you that you will be there forever: like Sisyphus and his rock, the only difference being that the gods left him alone while any second you could be called upon, from one of those doors, to defend yourself or die."

"You understand, Erin. Jenny never seemed to."

In silence they finished the tea and cookies. "Can we not go back yet?" Erin asked as they packed up and shook and rolled the blanket.

"Great. Where shall we go?"

"Over to the ocean."

They drove down to the last parking lot at Ocean Beach, parked, left their shoes on the bike's seat and climbed over a dune and down to the shore. The tide was on its ebb and the light through the sky's sharp clarity colored the wave foam so white that it was at first almost like looking directly into the sun. Being a Thursday in October, there were few people on the beach, and the further south they walked, where the dunes rose to block the coast highway, they came to a point where the shore was empty for as far as they could see.

"Did you ever try acid again?"

"Are you kidding?"

"No. A girl I know had a horrifying experience like yours and she decided she didn't want to go on living with the fear of it so she got with me and another really trusted friend and took acid again." Erin had drifted over and was walking in the final touch of the tide.

"And I suppose you'll tell me everything was just beautiful?"

"For her, yes. Maybe not for everybody. Some never recover. She was able to understand and really transcend that horrifying experience. And it taught her other things. I'm serious, Ted. It freed up so much garbage in her life too."

"Sounds like a miracle."

"She was ready. I know people who took acid scared to death and everything turned out all right for them. I'm not saying it's right, just telling you what I know."

They stopped and looked back toward the Cliff House Restaurant. It was so distant it looked like just undefined surfaces, some flashing intermittently when the sun reflected off the glass. "This was a beautiful idea, Erin." Ted gently reached out and grasped her hand and they started back.

"It was."

"I want to ask you something that may sound a little odd." She nodded. "How come it's so easy to be with you?"

"I feel the same, Ted." She put her free hand over his, like friends would who'd known each other a very long time.

During the next week, Erin received so many orders that she was working at the shop on her days off, and both the grade and complimentary remarks Ted received on his paper had motivated him to spend more time on reserved reading material and research which usually bought him home with just enough time to prepare his main meal before driving off to work.

On the Thursday after their picnic, Ted had a midterm in the morning and decided to do nothing when he got home around noon. He'd treated himself at Hanson's by picking up a pastrami and cheese, a side of cold slaw and a piece of their home made banana cream pie. He was working on the first half of the sandwich when Erin walked up from the corner carrying her bag and two bolts of material under her arm. She seemed tired.

"Do you have time for some tea?"

She put the material and bag on the porch's wall and sat down next to him on the top step. "Do you still have green?"

"You're the only tea drinker around here." He got up.

"I see you've been to Hanson's," she teased.

"A treat for acing my midterm. It felt very good."

"Your pastrami smells great."

"I've got the other half inside. Did you have lunch?" Erin shook her head.

"I just completed the last order. I'm caught up."

"How about I take the pastrami out and make it a cheese sandwich with coleslaw? Their homemade slaw is the best."

"Are you sure?"

"Yes."

"I am hungry. Banana and granola at six."

Ted prepared the plate and tea and carried them out with the tea bag still in the mug. She sipped it and tried the cold slaw. She sighed. "Delicious. Sinfully rich but delicious." She closed her eyes as if to enhance the taste. "The sandwich is good too," she laughed, "even without pastrami."

"You need some rest."

"It's hard with the stress at home the last few days. Lots of tension. I haven't told you but you'll be happy to know that Mark decided to go home and take his draft physical straight."

"How come?"

"There's some law where he can get his job back. And with his degree there's got to be something he can do besides kill people in the jungle. The military covers a lot of territory and different kinds of jobs." Erin broke off a piece of bread with cheese and put some cold slaw on it. "He kept going back and forth but it's settled. He leaves by bus on Saturday."

"How will you take up the slack in rent?"

"I don't know. We've also had Caroline and Ken separate. Her family has been really hard on her living with someone. Calling all the time, that sort of thing. Her father even threatened to get some kind of strong arm guy after Ken. She's upper middle class Cleveland and Ken's poor."

"What's their status now? I haven't seen the bike or either of them for a few days."

"Bike's in the shop. She flew home yesterday. Her mother just showed up suddenly."

"Wow. Where was I?"

"Probably at school. It happened like a flash. Ken came home from a split shift at the restaurant and didn't even know about it. My impression is that she may have wanted to go all along."

"What's he going to do?"

191

"The restaurant owner has a tiny studio upstairs where Ken can live and he wants him to learn the management side. I think he'll stay."

"What about you, Liz, Josh and Red Cloud?"

"It looks like they can buy a house on his G.I. Bill. I don't know what I want to do, Ted." She paused and looked at him and then up toward the imaginary summit of Mt. Davidson. "I'm never going to make a real living just sewing plus minimum wage as a clerk. I just can't charge what my time is worth."

"You're not thinking about going too?"

Erin reached out and touched his right hand, letting her fingers move slowly down to his finger tips and fall away. "I've been getting letters and calls from my Mom and Dad."

"But, the way they acted?"

"Things change. It hurt them. I understand. They had high hopes for me, more than pregnant at eighteen. Afterward, the way they acted, it was just stupid pride."

"You're more compassionate than I think I could be in the same situation."

"Maybe it's more that I miss them and my brothers. Cleveland's not so bad. Even some San Francisco kind of neighborhoods and hangouts. I've been thinking a lot about it lately."

"What would you do?"

"If I lived at home and got a part-time job I could maybe get my degree in design. We've got one of the best schools in the country, and my grades were good."

"Will you do something for me?"

She looked at him for a moment. "Big Sur, Ted?"

"As friends. A couple days. It would be a nice good-bye, if good-bye it may be."

"Friending."

"Friending?" he repeated.

"More than lovers or friends. But never good-bye."

As it happened, Erin did decide to leave at the end of October, only twelve days away. After their lunch, Ted found himself spending more days on the porch, bringing material home instead of reading in the library. He saw her only to wave to or when he helped them load Josh's VW bus for Ken's move. Soon, a little at a time, she was helping Liz move plants and pictures, all of Liz and Josh's small furnishings. Josh had gotten the G.I. loan on a small rundown three-bedroom row house out in the avenues.

He had first class mechanical skills, and Ted imagined that in a year or two it would be the nicest looking, best kept house on the block. How ironic that two semi-hippies with a boy named Red Cloud would come all the way from Cleveland to live in a little box on a street where probably no one knew what a Lakota was, or even thought of naming a child any name but Mike or Mary. He also knew that because the city was what it

193

was, they'd be drinking some wine or a beer over a barbecue at a neighbor's in no time at all.

By the following Sunday evening when Ted went off to work, the "commune," as he would always remember it, held only the essentials for living out the week. The plan was to move the following Saturday, the day after Erin was going back to Cleveland.

Monday night when he got home at twelve-thirty, Erin was asleep in her clothes on the futon. At her request, they were leaving right after he got off work. The moon illuminated her face pressed against a pillow. He knelt and gazed at her for a moment before she stirred and saw him. Her arms stretched out and he pulled her to a sitting position. "I'm ready."

Riding through Golden Gate Park, the moon's radiant light seemed to encompass all but the most distant stars. They turned south at the windmill and onto the empty highway. Erin held him, her hands in his down coat pockets, her hair blowing at the edges of the multi-colored wool hat she wore. Ken had loaned her his extra leather jacket and pants, and she felt the wind as Ted did, only on their cheeks.

From the height of the foam blowing off their crests, the waves looked enormous, walling up and breaking thunderously as the light seemed to dash like a surfer across their face, vanishing in the rush to shore. Neither spoke. Now and then they pressed against each other as the bike left the city behind.

After some hot chocolate in an all-night diner in the old section of Monterey's Cannery Row, they spotted a cloud formation out toward Pacific Grove. It stretched south and had a trailing mist down that way. By the time they passed Carmel, a light rain was falling.

It was just a drizzle when Ted turned off Highway 1. There were no lights anywhere, but he knew the cabin they were in and drove up the gravel road filled with moon shadows. The door was unlocked. There was a fire laid which he touched off, and by the time they'd unloaded and put away their gear the chill in the cabin was gone.

There was a shower stall almost too small to turn around in and a raised white 1920s tub with claw feet. She insisted he go first. He showered quickly and came out wearing a dark green sweat suit with a hooded top. The hot water had taken the edge off their trip and he felt tired and relaxed as he opened the bottle of red wine she'd carried in her bag. Two single beds, made up with pillows like studio couches, stood against the walls on either side of the fireplace, and a couch and much scarred coffee table of pine directly in front. The couch looked like it had come over on the Mayflower but was firm. Ted sat down with his wine in the dark.

Erin came from the bath into the firelight and he held up a glass of wine. She was in red long johns, and stood sipping the wine and watching the flames. He saw the outline of her body for the first time. "You're beautiful. I mean, your face was always beautiful."

She looked down at herself. "I'm happy with the way I look. Somehow that American hang-up passed me by." She settled in next to him and they watched and listened to the flames until their glasses were empty.

He patted her knee. "Which bed do you want?"

"By the window, if you don't mind."

"Be my guest. I'm going night-night." He helped her up and they hugged.

Ted was almost asleep when his head touched the down pillow, but he heard her voice come through the darkness. "Thank you for bringing me here."

He normally was a light sleeper, but when he awoke the room was full of sunlight. At first he couldn't place the sound, like a buzzing, and he sat up. Erin's bed was made. She stood at the stove in their tiny kitchen. It was separated from the rest of the room by the cedar bar with its smooth granite counter top and three stools.

"Morning."

"More like midmorning."

"You're kidding."

"Well, nine-thirty."

"I can't believe I slept through your getting up."

"I was very quiet. I walked down to the general store across the road. They've really got a big stock but all I brought back was breakfast: OJ, eggs, toast and granola from home." She was moving the scrambled eggs around a small pan. "I imagine you're a bacon eater, but I got Canadian. Less fatty. Tea and OJ are our only beverages I'm afraid."

He drank the OJ she'd poured and sat down on the first stool. "Tea's fine. Can't I do anything?"

"Sure. The dishes after breakfast. Then we'll go shopping."

"I'll pack us a lunch and take you on one of the hikes I discovered. I want to introduce you to the Johnson's."

"I met them at the general store. Really down home people. They like you."

"They let me rattle on about the divorce when I was here before."

They took the food outside and sat on a wooden swing that hung from the front porch rafters. Other than the sounds of the forest around them, it was as if they were alone. The stillness had its effect on their conversation, and they spoke only about Erin's breakfast and their surroundings.

He cleaned up the kitchen while she brushed her hair and made his bed. Then they walked to the general store and brought back enough to last them the three days until Thursday night. He had promised her a good-bye breakfast Friday morning in a special diner he knew in Salinas. She was flying out that afternoon.

After putting away the groceries, they spent the rest of the morning in the sun on the porch. Around noon, as promised, Ted made tuna, lettuce, tomato and avocado sandwiches. Erin still ate some chicken and fish. He had a small backpack which easily held the sandwiches, two oranges and water.

They took off up the gravel road. Since theirs was the last cabin, it was less than a quarter mile before the road ended and became a fairly wide trail that skirted the long sloping edge of a hill overrun with a ground cover flowering in shades of deep

197

red and orange amidst a fairly thick stand of young, newly planted redwoods. In little more than an hour of climbing slowly upward they came onto a ridge with more mature redwoods above and below them which filtered the sea beyond. They stopped for lunch by the last tree before the trail began to rise more steeply into grasslands.

"You make a good sandwich."

"Thanks. I learned cooking by osmosis. My mother was always pestering me to watch what she was doing in the kitchen. Some of it got through."

Erin looked at the water. From up where they were the waves could be seen forming, but they disappeared before breaking onto the unseen shore. She turned to him. "I would never have seen this."

"Well, you'll see more in the next two days. And maybe again."

She studied his face. "I hope so. But I have to go back now." He nodded in resignation. "I also have a confession to make and I hope you know that what I say is out of caring." He nodded again. "Mark gave me a cube of LSD, a very light dosage."

"I guess I'd be upset if it wasn't you and we weren't here. I know you did it out of caring, but, Erin, what would you do if I flipped again? You know what happened before."

"Ted, I can feel you...I can feel you want to try. And if you flipped I'd be the most miserably sorry and guilty person in the world because...." She hesitated, looking for the right words.

"I know you would."

"But I don't think it's going to be bad, Ted. I sense you want to know, to heal this if you can. And that's why it can be worthwhile."

He got up. A small fishing boat was passing a mile off shore. "I do." He ate the rest of his lunch standing, and after some water they trekked off up the trail which kept climbing, leveling off, dropping and climbing for another good hour or more until they reached a steep incline that instantly became more rocky. "We'd better turn back today. From the cabins to here it's about 2 and a half to three hours. If we descend, it's thirty minutes or so to the bottom of the gorge and then just a short way along the river bed. It's dry in summer and comes out under the highway to a virgin stretch of beach that's all but impossible to get to from the highway. Mr. Johnson told me about it. Come on, I promised you one elegant good-bye dinner in Carmel.

"I'll be ready for that after a deep soak in that tub."

They returned to the cabin by five-thirty as the twilight began. She'd brought one of her creations and put it on over her long johns for the ride. He had a turtle neck and cords so they were dressed up enough for the small and very old Mexican restaurant near the bottom of Carmel's main street where the stores and shops ended. It was hidden in a courtyard, and the weather, even without heat lamps, was still warm enough to eat outside. They sat at a secluded table for two in a far corner next to a small reflection pool and fountain which gave them a view of the entire courtyard, filled with tables, whose tile blended into the interior through open French doors. They ordered a good bottle of California Merlot, salads and two dinners consisting of chicken and cheese enchiladas, beans, rice and guacamole. Since it was a Tuesday night on the verge of the off season there was only one party of four, probably locals, on the far side of the courtyard.

After the waiter poured the wine and departed, Ted raised his glass. "Here's to your new life and dreams."

"And to yours." They toasted.

Erin had set her glass down and Ted touched it again with his. "Here's to wishing you would stay."

She looked into his eyes for a moment. "Forever?"

"You tell me." He touched her cheek with his hand.

"Doesn't it feel like forever now?"

"Yes. Truly."

They spoke quietly about the day and watched the fountain until the waiter crossed the empty courtyard with their dinner. Erin had eaten little Mexican cooking back home and she was impressed with its lightness and sauces that perfectly complemented each dish. They ate with the appetite and appreciation of two hikers.

"You've lived in San Francisco your whole life. Do you think this has been a special time or just more forgotten American History as usual, another unlearned lesson?"

She nodded. "Yes, but it has nothing to do with the dress, civil and women's rights or politics. It's difficult to define. It's more like an undercurrent."

200

"Like anticipation? That maybe the world could change for the better today, or tomorrow?"

Ted poured them more wine. "Yes. For me it's how I feel every day going to work at five. You pull out of the cable car barn and go downtown to Market Street. The streets are clean, empty, just a few taxis and delivery trucks. Breeze, my conductor, would spring for coffee and fresh sweet rolls, on the city of course, and we pick up a few domestics and other service people going up to the hotels. Everyone is off by the time we reach Nob Hill. We ride alone across the hills and down Hyde Street to Aquatic Park on the first light. The world at peace with itself. The Golden Gate and all that ocean, different every single day. Some days out there on the line it's dull, others, nothing but problems and you want to quit. But in there, once in a while, is a day you'd swear was made for you, just for you, by, I don't know, some deep presence looking out for you. Like the presence I feel, being with you."

Erin's fingers gently moved across the top of his hand. "I think that's forever."

"Me too. But dropping acid?"

"Could you call it a remedy?"

Ted shook his head. "I was the oldest, and supposed to be perfect even when I didn't know what that meant. Supposed to anticipate what it was, any given moment. And a lot of time I just didn't get it right, ending up disappointing my parents. It's illegal. That may be a stupid reason but that's what they taught me. That's what stuck."

"And lots of guilt?"

201

"Sure. Intellectually I know I'm no bad guy, no sinner, but…."

"After twenty-five years," she caressed his hand, "that's hard to shake."

"More like how. How do you throw out these crippling fears?"

"Maybe that's why we came out from Cleveland, each in our own way. We thought or imagined this new America where people wanted to share what the earth gave, do meaningful work, care for the planet and embrace each other with respect. No more competition and greed. No more killing each other here and abroad." She sighed through her smile. "Like creating a world at peace in Golden Gate Park." She laughed.

"With our windmill as corporate headquarters?" She laughed harder. "That's what it has all meant I think. But what has changed? It seems so simple, where everyone has a small plot of ground, enough food. A place of silence, where you don't go out into combat with each other." He picked up the check and shook it. "Well, the antiquated economics haven't changed."

"How strange that so many have been given a greater right to something so empty as paper and plastic exchange. Everybody should have the same right."

"That's what the undercurrent has been, to me. It's what I think everyone hoped for."

They walked up the street and looked into the shops. Few were still open but in one Ted found a plain copper American Indian made bracelet with a single polished turquoise set in it. He'd mail it to her. He was studying it so intently that when he looked up she was gone. In a moment she came from the rear of the shop. "The owner wanted to see my dress up closer. Wanted to order some. Oh, well."

"How'd she like the long johns?

"Thought the whole costume quite chic," she grinned.

The moon was behind scattered clouds but it broke through just before Big Sur. Back in the cabin, Ted lit the fire. They were in bed and asleep before its warmth filled the room.

About three-thirty, Erin felt an almost imperceptible pressure against her shoulder. Embers from the fire were the only light. "Are you all right, Ted?"

"I'm sorry."

She sat up. "That's okay." She moved over so he could crawl in beside her.

"I haven't slept much."

"Do you want to talk?"

"No. I want to hike out to the sunrise." She touched his forehead with her index finger. "If we get up now and pack a breakfast and lunch, we can be there around six-thirty. Sun's due up near seven." He paused and put his hand on hers, gently pressing it to his forehead for a moment. He got up and lit two candles on the hearth instead of lights. "I'm not sure."

"You don't have to decide now." She put her feet on the floor. "Do you want to start in the kitchen or bathroom first?" He could barely make out her smile in the candlelight.

Erin had turned on the one naked bulb in the kitchen and made two fried egg sandwiches, his with Canadian bacon, by the time he finished in the bathroom. "If you'll do a couple of your tuna specials, we'll have breakfast and lunch. There's a large bar of chocolate with almonds, four oranges and two apples."

While she used the bathroom, Ted made his sandwiches and laid everything out on the counter top next to his pack, along with a large old fashion canteen usually carried on a strap over a saddle horn.

"Where did you find that?"

"In the cupboard. I washed it with soap and hot water and nothing strange looking came out. If we carry that and the full bottle of orange juice we'll have enough liquids for the day. This canteen's better than the one on my bike."

She helped him pack. Each took a final swig of juice and she put it and the canteen in her hemp bag and hoisted it on her shoulder. "Not that heavy."

They headed out under a clear sky with the moon moving west above them. The hoot of owls in the trees far up the hill was vague, but they heard their boots leave the gravel and make a kind of hushed-breathing sound as they passed into the high grass.

The moon opened the night before them as they cleared the trees and came out on the ridge. Once, up ahead, something came down the hill and paused on the trail before dissolving into the trees below. "The creek is the natural drainage. There may still be a thin stream or at least standing pockets of water for local critters." They made good time across the ridge, and Ted stopped when the steeper descent began. "Our light'll be sporadic until we get to the bottom of this gorge. If you start to slip, I'll be right here to fall on." She laughed behind him. "It shouldn't be too bad a climb down."

When they reached the creek bed they paused to look up. On the side of the descent the land rose gently, but on the other it was a steep wall of rock. Above, the sky's first interchange between dawn and the moon had begun. Except for some odd stones, the creek bottom was dry, soft and easy to walk in though a small trickle of water ran along the side closest to the wall of rock. It appeared to be percolating from the stone.

In about a half hour they passed under the steel arch of the highway bridge and came out onto the beach. The dawn light was increasing as the darkness of the sea began to vanish in the illumination of waves breaking and rushing in on the high tide. Ted had found a place where the bluff came down to form a shallow, narrow, enclave of sandstone. This shelter was slightly elevated above the beach on a long easy rise of sand. They raked the area with branches and driftwood to level it out. Once their blanket was laid, they set out the juice, fruit, water, and egg sandwiches. Even cold, the eggs were good and the food and juice revived them as they sat in silence watching the surf.

"Erin?"

She took the cube, wrapped in foil, from her bag and unwrapped it, putting it in her palm. Erin was seated yoga style next to him with her legs crossed, right foot resting on her left thigh. She lowered her hands to her lap and studied his eyes. "I realize."

"I am really scared." He reached out and put his right palm into the instep of the foot resting on her thigh.

"Ted, I know you can do this. I'm with you. It's not going to be as rough as you think. I believe that. I'm with you."

"I feel?" He glanced at the sea. "Did you ever get lost from your mom in the store? Suddenly you look up and she was gone?"

"I know."

He raised his hand and slowly moved it above her foot until it hovered over her upturned palm which held the cube. Ted picked it up and brought it to him, hesitating. "Sun's almost up." He abruptly put it on his tongue and closed his mouth.

"It will take a little while to work, Ted. I'm right here. Just let it dissolve naturally. Try to concentrate on your breathing. Slow and easy, no hurry." She watched him. "That's it. It will bring you more to here and now, only this moment, with me, the beach, the sea, the breeze." She moved closer and held his hands with her right hand while gently massaging his neck with the left.

The first reflection of sunrise came from the east onto the water. The beach still lay in the disintegrating shadows of the bluff and mountains behind them. He took her hand in his. His grip wasn't tight but she knew it had begun. Erin wanted to reassure him.

What seemed to her like an hour later Ted released her hand, got up and ran slowly toward the bluing water. She hurried after him. But before he reached the tide he fell to his knees and stared at the sand for a long time until he started bending at the waist and rising up, bending and rising, his eyes open wide, surprised and frantic, like a small boy playing with an evil imaginary world. She knelt beside him. There were beads of sweat on his temples and forehead even with a breeze on the cool morning air. Erin felt the wetness on her neck and back and took off a sweater, but she didn't touch him. His body continued up and down like that for almost three hours until the movement turned to slow motion and, much later, stopped. Twice he had spoken in a whisper pushed forth each time by an enormous sigh, but she couldn't understand the words.

He watched the sea again for a long time. The perspiration began to evaporate and his gaze relaxed, but when he stood up, looking both ways, he seemed confused as if he didn't know where he was or why or what he must do. Erin felt his panic and flung her arms around him. "I'm here, Ted. With you." She held tightly, looking up into his face. "I'm here. I love you!"

His body shook for a moment and then went almost limp. Ted looked down and smiled as if he was just learning how to. "Erin."

She helped him back up to the blanket. He stopped twice to take long looks at the bluff and mountains above. The warm sun covered their camp site. Ted took some water from her and ate an apple.

"Would you mind doing what you were on my shoulders before?"

"Sure. Do you need anything?"

"No, thank you."

Erin massaged his shoulders until her hands were too sore to continue. All that time, he'd sat quietly, moving only to the pressure from her fingers. When she stopped and sat close, holding his hands, he began very slowly moving his head in every direction as if trying to see and see through everything around him. He had been doing this for a long time when the first of the sun's rays covered the remainder of the shore where they sat by the bluff. They stripped down to tee shirts and shorts and took off their hiking boots, feeling the warming sand on their feet. It was just past noon.

"It's so much," he said, breaking the long silence.

"Yes, Ted. It will be winding down now. A really light dose."

His hand circled the air around them. "You can hear the sunlight humming. Everything is so, what, original? That sounds dumb. Birds. Sea. Sand and wind. Right here. This is all there is or needs to be. It. That presence. I don't know where. It. 'One without a second' Shankara called it." He turned and looked at her. "Thank you."

"I told you you'd make the crossing."

"But I needed you. Even when I was back in that cage at the beginning and they were going after me and I thought I was going to die. Even then I knew you were there. Something keeping you there, here. I didn't even care if I died then."

"I hoped you'd know."

"You were there," Ted reassured her.

"I prayed for that. Meditated on it."

"Thank you, thank you." He leaned over and kissed her. "Do you think we can eat now? I'm starved." Their laughter lifted quietly into the bluff.

They ate everything except for the two oranges. The sun was high and unclouded and they basked in it until Ted fell sound asleep. Erin was very tired but she sat and watched his slow, relaxed breathing and the sea.

It was mid-afternoon when he awoke. Before they started back all he said was, "I'll tell you all, when I can."

The sun's descent was complete long before they got back to the cabin. After setting the fire and bathing, they drank some wine and Erin warmed two cans of tomato soup with milk and some crackers. They lay in the beds, talking until first Erin and then Ted fell quietly to sleep. It wasn't even eight o'clock.

The next morning they were awakened by a knock at the door. Ted answered.

"Morning, Ted. Sorry if I woke you."

"No, that's okay, Mr. Johnson. We hiked over the ridge yesterday. Pretty tired. What time is it?"

" 'Bout ten. Reason I came up was, thought you might like some fresh caught salmon. My son brought it in from down south last night." He offered up a brown package. "Three quarter pound. Enough for two."

"Thanks. Let me pay you."

"Nah. Thought you and the wife might like it." He winked, turned and went down the porch stairs to the path.

Ted put the salmon in the refrigerator. He glanced over at Erin but her bed was empty. He made tea and was trying to figure out breakfast when she came around the counter top. "How'd you sleep?"

"Quietly," she smiled. Her long hair was now in a single braid. "The real question is you."

"I'm very good today. No flashbacks so far. I almost think I won't be having many. Feeling very light."

She squeezed his shoulder and opened the refrigerator. "How about an apple cut in two, the trail mix we forgot to take yesterday, tea and the second bottle of OJ?"

"Perfecto. I thought we'd hang around here a while and drive down to Napenthe's for a long lunch. Sit outside, a bottle of wine, most breathtaking view on this side of the planet. Then maybe, a long walk on some empty beach."

After the light breakfast, they walked down to the general store and wandered the aisles looking over the variety of goods. The twice weekly shipment of fresh fruit and vegetables had come in earlier and Erin decided they'd have small red potatoes and asparagus with the salmon for dinner. Ted picked out a bottle of Pouilly Fuisse. He had no idea what it tasted like but the owner's wife recommended it with salmon. Erin asked if he'd like some dessert and he replied that he couldn't conceive of anything more unhealthy, so she bought a half pint of locally made vanilla ice cream and a slice of homemade pecan pie she decided they would divide. Noon had come by the time they put everything away and picked up the highway going south.

It was warm enough not to wear coats, and they drifted through the curves cross-cut with shadows of pines, redwoods

210

and the hills rising steeply from the highway. The distance was short and there were few cars in the parking area at Napenthe's. Strolling across the broad, open terrace, miles of the south coast opened before them. The sunlight at that hour cast the water in a blue with the green patina of copper fittings on an old leather trunk. The restaurant was empty except for a dozen tables by the windows high above the sea.

They ordered Caesar salads with hot French bread and a half liter of white house wine, and sat alone on the terrace with the long bench facing the south coast as their table. There were two weathered, wooden chairs that hadn't yet been taken in for the season's end.

"When I look down there, I think I'd like to be a bird in my next life, or for a few hours right now."

"Me too." He reached over and stroked the back of her neck. "But right now I am thinking more about landing."

"You mean when the plane's wheels touch twice before you know you're down?"

He grinned. "Yeah, but more like jumping from a moving cable car and being sure my legs'll be moving fast enough when I hit the ground so I don't stumble and break my neck."

"Did it help then? I didn't want to ask, sorry."

"Next to these hours with you, it was the second most powerful moment so far. But if I wrote it down it wouldn't fill half a page. There were the colors, the intensity everyone speaks of....but then everything seemed to dissolve into this painfully bright light out of which unfolded the jungle, the clearing and me in the cage. They kept poking and trying to spear me. No mercy. I was bloody and terrified. Yet I knew vaguely that you were there somewhere. But I couldn't reach out and touch you or the sand, the surf. I kept bending and sitting up in the cage, but I couldn't dodge them. At one point I really thought I'd bleed to death and I called out as loud as I could for my parents. Utterly nuts, right?

"Well, the second time I called I was instantly alone in the cage. Everyone was gone. Something told me to stand up and I stumbled weakly to my feet. As I did, the cage just broke up in a hundred pieces and I collapsed. I sat there not knowing what path to take. Then I felt someone holding me, and your voice saying 'Ted, I'm here.' As I looked up, your beautiful face came into mine and though the jungle and cage were still there they seemed to disintegrate and I was left with you, the sea and the beach.

"I don't really know what it all meant. Obviously the childhood stuff. But I also knew that it didn't matter. That my parent's dreams had died before they were thirty and they wanted to live mine and couldn't. Their demands were nothing more than them crying out, wanting to live an authentic life through me. Unintentional hurt, like theirs, can be healed. I know that now. Forgiveness, we save for our enemies only."

Erin was crying softly, but not from anger, frustration or despair. "I understand too." She tried to smile.

He nodded. "So simple once it falls from the head to the heart. But what a hell of a tough journey to make sometimes. I took the pill and we both learned. How do you figure that?"

She reached over and kissed his cheek. "That means we don't need any hand-me-down lives. Don't have to put up with them. Maybe even find a way to live with integrity in this world overwhelmed by grief. I think that's what the 'sixties' were all about. And some are still trying and will keep trying by passing it on to their kids and others they meet." She got up and straddled his legs and settled in his lap, hugging him.

"We'll try for the authentic." He returned the kiss. "How about we ride down the coast for an hour or so and find another beach so you can teach me. I may never learn to meditate but I might learn to sit still."

When they returned at dark to the cabin, it was as if they'd been together for a life time. They ate and enjoyed Erin's special dinner. Afterwards, they moved their mattresses in front of the fire place, pushed away the table, and pulled down the couch cushions to prop themselves up. In sweats and long johns they lay watching the fire.

"Ted, what will you do?" Erin asked.

"Try to keep myself as close to the moment, the one that's happening right now, wherever I am. Try to find my work in this life."

"I will too."

213

The First Dialogue

I

As she entered the kitchen, the North Star swayed like a dot of white oil paint the size of a .002 brush in the November darkness against the mirage of dawn. The coffee maker, set for five-thirty, was gurgling faintly and far off where the tile counter ended and the breakfast room began with its glass and steel table and four chairs silhouetted now in the first light from the tinted sliding glass doors that opened onto a small redwood deck. The view spread down across the Haight District's old houses and over the eucalyptus and pine trees of Golden Gate Park's Panhandle where it rose in the random lights on waking streets to end as a thin bank of fog out to the north in Pacific Heights.

Jenny poured a half cup and carried it gratefully to the table. She turned the chairs, using one as a footrest, to face the star. It had become just about her only time to herself since moving in with Jerry five months ago, because besides working toward her MA in Fine Art, like it or not she was at twenty-three nearly the mother of his twins, Jane and Jerry Jr., the "4 J's" as his friends called them.

She put down the cigarette she was about to light. Jerry chain smoked, and it had become her habit not out of liking but in self-defense against smoker's kiss. Now she smelled as bad as Jerry in the morning.

Jenny watched the star dimming as the dawn light grew in the distant view, the yard and the breakfast room. Dim or bright, the star was a memory whose essence would never exist again because, for all practical purposes, it had slowly diminished in these past months. In seven more her divorce from Ted would be official, final.

During the best times, the North Star had been the reflection through which she and Ted had seen each other. That was all of '66 when they first met, and most of '67 when they were married with him finishing as a senior at Berkeley and her as a junior at SF State. But when he returned from Vietnam in '68, they slowly grew out of the pleasure of sitting at their kitchen table, drinking cheap red wine and talking dreams, desires and ambitions until the star rose and, under its light, they finally fell asleep on the big futon. From the day he took the job driving a cable car she felt the star receding as if into another galaxy where neither of them could follow. She studied the stove's clock. Five-fifty. Ten or fifteen minutes, then the day.

Jenny got up, poured coffee and sat down again. The cigarette was lying by its half empty pack and she stared at it as the coffee warmed her. Finally, she reached for it. The smoke spread around her, momentarily blunting the view.

Ted had come back a smoker from Vietnam. She had asked him to go outside, either the back stairs or front porch. Even when the weather turned cold and rainy, he never complained, and this somehow angered her.

What was he doing now? She'd run into him a few times on campus. So odd that he was taking an Oriental Studies class, a subject in which he'd never expressed interest. And he'd stopped smoking. That was all she knew. She'd learned that the

215

second time when they stopped to talk outside the Commons. Afterward, she had felt resentment, even anger, because in those few short months he was no longer so contrite about their breakup. God, how he'd cried when she told him about Jerry. But how could he have been so surprised, he had become abstract and inattentive? She'd tried to talk about it. But they ended up just going through the motions of marriage.

In these past five months Jenny had more than once felt the twinge of remorse in the way she'd handled it. "I want a divorce, Ted. I can't be here anymore."

"But why?"

"Because I don't think you're here, and haven't been for a long time," she'd blurted in anger. "Ever since you came back we've just been disintegrating. First you decide to drive a cable car after all we'd ever talked about before you got drafted was law or investments. But I accepted your decision, didn't I? I would have gotten a job to get you through law school. Anything."

"Yes, I know that."

"And I was so damn disappointed. You weren't there when I told my folks. It just knocked them for a loop."

"I realize that." It had been early afternoon in their kitchen with the sun through the three cornered windows so bright that everything, including themselves at the table he'd built, took on a nearly blinding white radiance. Across from him, her face seemed like particles of light in flux, her features blurring and clearing before him. "But, I told you then, law, investments, the whole unending business-profit thing seemed so utterly empty after I got out of Vietnam. And still does. I'm

216

sorry. Look, I can change. Just, please don't leave," he had pleaded.

"Don't you realize it's too late?"

"It's that guy, Jerry, your drawing instructor from last year, isn't it?" She nodded.

"He's years older than you, Jenny." He looked out the window, but she saw his tears. "How long?"

"Almost...three months."

"You, you were...and here with me?"

"You and I haven't made love for longer than that. Look, I'm sorry I've hurt you. I know I have, badly. I'm...I've just got to take responsibility for my life, what I want and need. When someone does that, there can be pain. You know that. None of this is really a surprise is it?"

"Your therapist at school been telling you this stuff?"

"What does it matter? We grew apart. You never asked me about my art anymore. Hardly looked at any of the work that I'd bring home. You used to be so enthusiastic and supportive. You didn't even want to go to the end of the year student show."

"I'll do better, Jenny. Please, let's just try a little longer?"

"I can't. Jerry makes me feel wanted when I'm with him, when he holds me."

"But I always tried to be kind, caring."

"Yes, before you were drafted, before they let you out on that medical thing. After, when you got back, then I felt more like a housekeeper than a lover. I kept hoping, Ted, but nothing changed. And don't tell me you didn't know. I tried to talk about it but you weren't listening."

"For three months you've been with this Jerry asshole and never said anything?"

"He's not an asshole, he makes love to me. Do you understand?"

The cigarette had burnt itself out on the saucer of her cup. Again, the clock. It was 6:05. The day had come.

II

Jenny had made lunches for herself and the children by the time Jerry entered the kitchen. He carried the morning paper and brushed his hand across her shoulder in passing, taking his coffee to the table where she'd cut up a small bowl of fruit for each of them and put out cereal, milk and toast with butter, jam and peanut butter.

"How'd you like the party? He asked.

"I don't know. I think they somehow can't get over seeing me as your 'student'."

He lit a cigarette and began eating the fruit. "You graduated, remember?"

"But, now I'm a graduate student."

"You know how academics are. Even in the fine arts."

Jenny sat down in her North Star chair and ate her fruit. "Yes, but that won't deter me from teaching."

"Then flee the academy." He laughed and coughed like someone with an advanced lung disease.

"Jerry?"

"What? I'm okay. My last x-rays were 'A' number one. By the way," he patted the top of her hand before he started another cigarette off the one he was smoking and she tried not to notice the tobacco stains on his index and middle fingers. "I'm sorry about last night. What with the party and such a long day. Hey, my romantic notions weren't what they should be. Also, I'll admit I'm always worried about the kids suddenly appearing at the door."

"I know."

"Oh, look, I hate to ask, and I know it's another of many impositions, but I need you to pick up the kids from soccer practice today. I just glanced at my calendar. I totally forgot about the special faculty meeting tonight at five."

"Jerry, come on. It's my one day of the week I can put four hours together in the studio."

"I know. I promise I'll make it up to you."

"Sure." He leaned over and she turned her cheek for him to kiss.

"I'm sorry, Jenny."

"This romance has turned into a marriage pretty quickly." Jenny tried to make it sound light.

"Hey, marriage? Freedom first, correct? A little freedom for both of us."

"Look who has all the freedom."

He poured cereal and milk in the empty fruit bowl. With his cigarette resting on the plate beneath, it looked like the cold food was steaming. "Come on, Jen, you know what my schedules like this semester with teaching overload plus a faculty committee assignment. I'll try to make it better next semester and take some pressure with the kids and all off of you." Jerry ate his cereal fast as he glanced at the paper.

"Jerry, this situation with my folks has really been bugging me."

"Not that again?"

"Yes, that again. I've got to mend this with them somehow."

"They know people live together. They don't object to your older brother doing it, right?"

"Because they know he'll be getting married. And she's his age."

He snapped his fingers. "Damn. I also forgot. The seminar in L.A. was moved up to next weekend."

"What about the kids?"

"I cleared it with Margo. She'll take 'em the whole week so you will be a woman of leisure."

"Why can't I go with you?"

"Budget, business and, I guarantee, boredom. I'm on the run from dawn until sometimes after midnight."

"I could entertain myself."

'What about your own art, studio time?" He lit another cigarette and went back to reading the paper.

III

Margo, Jerry's ex, didn't pick up the children until late the following Sunday afternoon, and he had flown to the L.A. seminar that evening. On Monday, Jenny attended class and spent the whole day painting in the graduate school studio. Only one student came in at lunch, but left in an hour, so she had the studio to herself the entire afternoon. The weather for November had remained warm, and Jenny opened the large glass doors in the studio's south wall of windows. The breeze from the enclosed Japanese patio and garden carried in the fresh air. Though she tried to shake it, a feeling of self-consciousness clung to her all day. Only as the light in the patio and studio began to fade did she realize that she didn't have to be anywhere for anyone. She even detoured going home to pick up a Black Forest Ham and American cheese sandwich with homemade cold slaw and a piece of cherry pie from Hanson's Café.

Getting home about six-thirty, she cleaned the entire house and then showered for half an hour. It was nine-thirty when she took the food to the breakfast room. She left the lights off there and in the kitchen. The street lights beyond the house were dull and distant in the mist gathering across her view of the city.

Jenny couldn't see much to the east because Mt. Sutro curved outward in its landscape of houses and trees. But as if gazing through the hill, she could imagine almost in detail the ancient rectangular pile of brick that was Franklin Hospital. Beyond, the Noe Valley ascended in its rows of wood and stucco houses and apartment buildings. Once, she had climbed to the roof of their old place over there where Ted still lived. He had worried about her safety and gotten upset when she'd seen him on the sidewalk three floors below and called out. Nothing seemed too risky that first married year, and for three summer days she'd tried to paint the hills rising to the east and south above her. She painted it just as hills: soil, natural plants, and stands of cedar, Cyprus, redwood and pine. Maybe a cabin or two, foot paths and a dirt road. That was all, the way she hoped it had been long ago. But she never finished it. He had gone into the military. If she had, it would have been Ted's birthday gift that year.

Jenny took a large bite from the sandwich, then the slaw. She'd never liked slaw until Ted introduced her to Hanson's homemade. They'd eaten at least one meal a week there, sometimes two. Now he probably went more often. She ate very slowly, loving the emptiness and quiet; all the motions and interactions of the house were gone. Maybe she would drive over to Hanson's for breakfast or dinner one day this week. She knew the whole family who owned it and could sit in a booth for two in the rear.

When she finished her meal, it had grown darker with an incoming fog and the quarter moon had vanished. She sat there until nearly eleven. When she finally crawled into bed it occurred to her that she had not smoked a cigarette all day.

IV

She awoke in the five o'clock darkness and, though she had no classes, got up immediately and dressed in jeans, a wool turtleneck and fleece lined wind breaker. With just a couple swallows of orange juice and no coffee she drove across town to Bay Street and parked in front of the Buena Vista Café across from Aquatic Park Plaza and the cable car turntable.

It was hardly six, but the restaurant side of the café was just opening, and she got black coffee and a sweet roll fresh and hot from the bakery and went across to sit in the gazebo by the turntable. There was no reason to be there. She had no clear idea why she had come.

A cable car pulled away and disappeared around the corner, going up Hyde Street. She sat for several moments until another one stopped on the incline next to the Buena Vista where one passenger got off before the car came down through the curve and rolled onto the turntable. The conductor and gripman got off and pushed the car around and into place for the return trip.

The black gripman wore a black leather vest and a blue uniform shirt with outlandishly puffy sleeves, and she knew that it was Breeze, Ted's friend and longtime conductor. He saw her, waved and sauntered over with his own coffee and roll. They hugged and she smelled the imported cologne she always remembered when he'd come over for dinner or the three of them went up to North Beach to the Jazz Workshop or the little Mexican place with the classical guitarist and Flamenco dancer in the storefront up by the Broadway tunnel.

Breeze put down his coffee and roll and held her hands. "Jenny, you look very good. Maybe a little tired but real good."

"I thought you wouldn't recognize me."

"Come on, foxy lady like you?" He smiled with his whole face. "What is it, four months?"

"Going on five." They sat down.

"How's it been, girl?"

"Busy. How come you're gripping not conducting?"

"They were shorthanded. Now that I work both ends it's more OT for me."

"You'll never rest."

"Try not to." His conductor rang the bell. "Gotta go."

"Is Ted...?"

"He punked out on me last sign up and went to nights after you two split. Four to midnight now, but still on the Hyde line." He pulled her up and they hugged again. "Can I do anything for you, Jenny?" She shook her head. "Okay, stay cool." He started back for the cable car.

"Breeze?" He stopped and turned back. "When is he off?"

"Thursdays and Fridays. You got a message for him I can deliver?"

"No."

She watched him round the curve and pull back on the grip. They waved to each other until he was out of sight behind the Buena Vista building.

Jenny went straight to school and the studio. Except for a lunch break in the Commons, she painted until after three.

It was past four when she found a parking space down by the Maritime Museum and walked back by the old chocolate factory, crossing over to the gazebo. A car was on the turntable, its cabin and outer benches only partially filled with tourists. The gripman and conductor stood apart on the wharf side of the little plaza where a bed of dead summer flowers separated them from a lawn rolling down towards the west end of Fisherman's Wharf. The gripman wasn't Ted. Jenny sat on a bench just outside the gazebo and waited.

The cable cars came and went in shorter intervals as more were added to the line for rush hour. With each car, Jenny tried to ignore the tension in her throat and the chill in her fingers that remained cold inside her fleece lined pockets. Finally, a car rolled onto the turntable and Ted got off. As he went around the car, she ducked into the gazebo and looked the other way until, a few minutes later, she heard the bell ring and he was headed downtown again. When it was out of sight, she hurried to her car and drove to Jerry's.

She warmed up with a dish of chili from a dinner made the previous week and ate it with a small salad and corn tortillas. By the time she'd finished and cleaned up it was dark. She drove back to the wharf.

Arriving at close to six-thirty, the rush hour was long over and Aquatic Park Plaza was lit by tall antique street lamps on delicately ornate poles which surrounded the plaza. Only four or five passengers sat waiting on the empty cable car. Ted's car was the third that came. This time she walked over and stood on the fringe of the revolving table. She smiled as he came around with the car's rotation.

Ted barely smiled back, and was about to push the car off and stop it when the conductor nodded that he would do it. Ted walked over. "Is something wrong, Jenny?" he asked, cautiously touching her sleeve but letting his hand drop quickly away.

"No."

"I mean…"

"He went to L.A. for a week and his kids are with their mother." She pushed her hands deeper into her pockets. "Oh hell, Ted. I don't know why I'm here."

"Your neighborhood's still a little ragged a few blocks closer to the park. Maybe you should stay with your folks."

"I'm fine. Besides, I'm kind of the wayward daughter."

"I'm sorry."

"I'm going to go over one day this weekend, maybe when my mom's home alone, and talk."

"She called me last month." He looked at his watch and then the cable car.

"What did she want?"

"Just see how I was doing. Talk."

"They always really liked you. She say anything about me?"

"Said you were a very bad child." Jenny looked instantly hurt but Ted grinned suddenly.

"I forgot about you." She tried to keep the hurt look but it didn't work.

"Still funny after all these months," he signed and looked at his watch again. "I have to go."

"Okay, bye."

"Jenny?"

"Go on, I'll see you."

"If you want to talk, I'll be out at the library tomorrow. How about lunch at the Commons?"

"You sure?" He nodded. She hesitated.

"Well?"

"Would twelve-fifteen be okay?"

"See you then." He climbed aboard, rang the bell, released the brake and pulled the car around the curve and across Bay Street. Jenny stood and listened until its metallic sound had vanished.

The next day was more like early October with a full sun on a light breeze. She had arrived early and bought some salami sandwiches with Jack cheese, chips, two milks and apples from the cafeteria. Most of the courtyard's stone tables and benches were sparsely occupied just before noon, and she chose one on the outer edge where she could watch for him coming down the wide cement walkway that meandered through the campus.

She'd just laid out the napkins and food when he came onto the walk by a side path. They both waved. She noticed how he walked, like he had in one of the first anti-war marches up Market Street; there was a formal, almost military gait to his stride but his arms swung loose and relaxed. They'd been assigned at random to carry a banner together in the center of the march. It was their first meeting.

"Morning." His smile made her feel they did this often, but the tightness remained in her throat though her hands had warmed up.

"Lunch is on me."

"Looks good." They opened the small bags of chips and the sandwiches.

"Don't worry, not homemade." Her smile was cautious.

"What do you mean? You cook very well."

Jenny shrugged. "Remember that first march we were in? I guess like our first date too?"

"Our first march, my last."

"Which became our first big argument later when I wanted us to be in the NOW march with the Gay and Lesbian Coalition."

"God, do I."

"Well, we'd only known each other a short time." She reflected a moment. "I can't even remember a worse argument ever, all the time we were together."

"Me either," he laughed.

"I was really pissed. And I thought it was the dumbest reason. Do you feel the same now?"

"More so. I hated crowds then and after Vietnam I never wanted to be in another."

"I could have been more tolerant," she said in reflection. "It wasn't that big a deal really, and I could have gone alone."

"Oh, you had a right to be upset. How's your work with NOW doing these days?"

"I resigned as campus president after I moved in with Jerry."

"What, he doesn't like the feminist movement?" She shrugged. "I guess I was okay on that score then?"

Classes had broken and the noon crowd began to stream in and out of the Commons. He looked at her. She'd grown her dark brown hair longer again. Her light olive complexion looked almost pale.

"You were actually more than okay. I didn't know it then."

"I felt for a long time it was pretty much all my fault, you know?" He watched the crowd for a moment. "For weeks, most of the summer, I went around trashing myself pretty good."

"I'm sorry. I know I tried to make you feel bad. Guilty. I was awfully insensitive. Just lately I realized…you going out there to the war, that LSD nightmare, the dead, being in the hospital, medical discharge, all of it. How could anyone with an ounce of sensitivity not come back changed?

"There's a girl in one of my classes whose brother went over. We were doing this assignment, a pencil sketch of what the war meant to us. She drew this naked young man with his legs apart and arms open like the Leonardo Di Vinci figure. You know the one I mean? But it was headless. Just this neck with a strangely shaped cartoon cloud above with two overlapping scenes inside. In the one on the right was a jungle scene; there was this soldier in combat gear carrying a machine gun and stepping into the scene on the left. Over there was a dining room where a dad, mom, two sisters and this same soldier, now dressed in slacks and a shirt, were eating Sunday dinner.

"My friend said that's how her brother came back. One day he was in the jungle fighting to stay alive and a few days later home at Sunday dinner. As if nothing had happened. As if that transition was just perfectly normal. You know what his

230

father said when they met him at the airport? Nothing. Just something like, 'How are you? How's it going?' Never asked him anything, never said another word about it." Jenny was leaning towards him, her brown eyes wide open under dark furrowed eyebrows. She caught herself and leaned back, drinking a little milk.

"Jenny, don't blame yourself. It happened on both sides. You talked to me a lot when I returned. I just didn't respond very well, that's all. It couldn't be fixed right then for either of us. For a long time, I didn't want to admit that, but I do now."

She hesitated before answering. "Yes. I guess so." They turned from each other to watch the lunch crowd thinning as quickly as it had begun. Some grey marine clouds kept changing the light as they passed over the sun. "But maybe it had nothing to do with that, the war, the Age of Hope as you've always called it. Maybe there was nothing to fix." The loud speakers on the library roof did their imitation of tower bells chiming, followed by a single gong.

"What do you mean?"

"I don't know exactly, Ted. Maybe before you went to Vietnam we were being more like others wanted us to be instead of as we really were. If we even knew what that was. Maybe we never started to really know each other for what we were until after you came home."

"Jenny, I'm sorry, but I have to get home and study a little before work. I'd like to talk more about that." He got up. "Thanks for lunch. I enjoyed it. How about coffee?"

"Tomorrow?" Her smile came and went so quickly he wasn't sure she had.

"Fine. Around eleven?" She nodded.

Ted arrived first. The courtyard was empty except for the stone tables and benches littered with plastic utensils, coffee cups and plates. Each time the breeze came up they would roll or slide closer to the edge, some falling onto the concrete beneath while soiled and unused napkins sailed forth, caught momentarily on the wind, like kite riding monks leaping from granite overhangs into the up draft of Tibetan canyons.

She came from the Commons carrying a new sketch pad, books, and a handbag under one arm and coffee in the other. "I figured you'd get some."

He took the pad and her shoulder bag and set it down for her. "I'm starting to drink a little tea."

As she settled on the stone bench opposite him her long dark hair caught the midday light. It was freshly washed and combed out wet. Jenny fussed with her stuff but didn't look at him. When she finally did, he was staring at her. "What, Ted?"

"You aren't wearing any makeup except a little lipstick. Like old times."

"You mean, before Jerry?"

He nodded. "I always said your lashes and eyebrows were dark enough not to need any." Jenny drank some coffee but didn't reply. "At any rate, I think it's a great look."

"Natural?" He laughed.

"Yes."

She pulled another new book from her shoulder bag and studied the cover for a minute then pushed it away. "How's the Oriental philosophy coming?"

"Interesting, but at this point it all seems to mesh together. Like everything overlaps. I guess the concept of the Divine Energy, God, can be called by dozens of names, but you can't reinvent it like a new wheel. I'm glad I'm taking it though."

"Are you still liking the cable car work?'

"Yes. Pay's good and my overhead is close to monastic." He smiled.

"In more ways than one?" she kidded. "Sorry, that was thoughtless."

"No, it's true," he confessed good naturedly, "but I did get to know a really extraordinary girl, for a short time. You remember the group that rented Tom's and Will's remodel?"

"Sure"

"And Erin, the dressmaker and designer?"

"The balloony dresses?"

"Beautiful fabrics and colors."

"They were, I admit."

"She just started stopping over now and then for a chat on the steps. It was nice. She was easy to be around. A quality. I can't describe it very well. Easy going, I guess. I felt very at ease with her."

"But it was short?"

"About a month. At the very end I took her to Big Sur for three days. Just last month. After you left I started taking these long solo rides: Petaluma, Big Sur, Santa Cruz Mountains around Ben Lomand, places like that." He looked at Jenny. Her face seemed to move toward sadness but turned to gaze up the campus walkway before it did. "What?"

Jenny ran her hand straight back through her hair a couple of times and shook her head as if to settle it back in place. "I've never thought of you in that way. You know, a real physical relationship, sex, making love to someone else. Modern me, huh? Pretty stupid. It's just, when we were together, especially before, when I felt so close to you. We'd go out and I'd see girls sort of make a play for you, come on to you at parties. I always knew it would be us together at the end of the evening."

"I'd like to tell you Erin and I had hour after hour of hot sex, unending passion. You know why? How do you think I felt when you left?" He roughly brushed away some tears with his shirt sleeve.

"Ted, I'm sorry. Please don't."

"No, just listen for a minute. I could have been unfaithful to you lots of times after going to work on the cars. Every day there's an opportunity. But I would never have been unfaithful. And not because of guilt and religious dogma. No. It was always about trust, the fact we'd been together a year, whether officially or not. I wanted it to work for us, in every way." It surprised him when he saw her tears and extended a napkin.

"Ted, I've always regretted…I'm so sorry for what I said the day I left. You know, about how you had no technique? How Jerry held me, made me feel. That was so ugly and cruel."

"You'd always seemed happy."

"Yes, before they sent you to Vietnam. I was. Very." Jenny blew her nose. The tears had almost stopped. She suddenly reached over and briefly squeezed his hand.

"That was a big ego hit. Hurt bad. But I figured it was my fault, completely. Yet I honestly didn't know what you meant. What I hadn't done for you."

"I was striking out, very angry. Now, well, I don't even think there is such a thing as technique. More and more I think it was just one of those beside the point ideas I was starting to talk about yesterday. Like the war, the Age of Hope, the proper thing to do and say. Somehow in a relationship all that seems beside the point." The loud speaker bells chimed and then gonged twelve times. "Oh, shit. Class. Do you understand?"

"I think. I'm not sure."

"Please, can we go on?"

"Sure, Jenny."

"Could you come for dinner tonight?"

"I work tonight. Tomorrow night I took my run on overtime, I have to work. You'd be happy. I actually started a little investment portfolio with my overtime. Mr. Junior Stockbroker, etc."

She smiled. "How about Friday?"

235

Ted got up with her and they strolled up the central walkway. "I don't want to be there, Jenny." She nodded in understanding, dabbing away the last of her tears. He sighed. "Look, what if I pick you up Friday around five? I'll make us dinner. You can bring dessert and a bottle of wine."

"Me, come there?"

V

The orange winter sun had moved away from the Presidio and beyond the Golden Gate Bridge when Ted needled his way across town by side streets and stopped in front of her house. An old man sitting in the gathered twilight of his porch up the block put down his newspaper to watch Ted climb the steps to the maple door, hand carved in an incoherently dense pattern on the bottom half as if the sculptor had given up at that point.

Jenny had made an old standard of theirs, tapioca pudding. The wine was a late '50s she confessed to taking from Jerry's wine rack.

By the time they returned and Ted had started the brown rice, made a soy and garlic based sauce, cut up the pork and a dozen vegetables, the sky was just an orange light touched with an open fan of clouds on the far hill above Franklin Hospital which resembled an abandoned medieval castle whose turrets had crumbled in the harshness of many winters.

Jenny was in the other room, but there was a bourbon and ginger ale on the dining table by her seat that she was

236

sharing with Ted. "You're a much better housekeeper than I was," she called.

"Not true."

"I never did like this décor, but I think I do now, after all the clutter I'm living with. And not a whole lot of dusting here." She laughed and was quiet. He heard her walk off the Oriental rug onto the hardwood. She opened and closed first the closet in the entry and then the bathroom door. She came under the kitchen arch and sat back down, taking a long sip from the glass.

Ted pointed toward a cupboard. "I keep the spirits and wine in there now, if you want to pour us another."

Jenny made them another drink, offering it to him, and sat back down. "I thought I was just going to have an anxiety attack in there. No kidding, my stomach got tight and I started feeling really cold."

"How are you now?" He had finished sautéing the meat and longer cooking vegetables and set them in a bowl in the oven before throwing on the softer ones, sprouts, squash, onions and peppers.

"Better."

"Bad memories, probably."

"Not all. I don't know what it was. Could we go back to where we left off? About what happened to Erin?"

"They all moved out. She went back to Cleveland. She hopes to go to a design school there. Said it was a good one."

"It is. I know the one she's talking about. By the way, I saw Larene a few days ago on campus. Eduardo got into the university down there. He really misses us all, and the city."

"I think he's better off in El Salvador than the draft."

Ted took the bowl from the oven and poured the pork, carrots and green beans in with the rest. He put the lid on the skillet. "I'll let it simmer a minute or two." By the time he'd opened and poured the wine, the stir fry was ready. He served it over the brown rice in bowls with chop sticks, and sat down next to her where they faced the windows. They raised their glasses. "Jenny. There was no sex."

"You didn't have to tell me."

"Come on, be honest?"

"Well."

"I know I didn't have to tell you."

She used her chop sticks skillfully. Their usual dinners out, other than Hanson's, had been either Chinese or Mexican. "You always did make terrific stir fry. Much better than me.'

"On this one dish, I'd have to say you're right."

"I don't know why I'd be so damned old-fashioned about this Erin relationship. Look at me after all, a lover and mother wrapped into one."

"We mostly talked down there at Big Sur. On my motorcycle rides, I found this little place with about a dozen small cabins. The owners built them one at a time. They're totally isolated from each other in the trees. Fireplaces. Kitchen.

You might like it. And, yeah, sure, we held each other. I even took acid with her again."

"God, no, Ted. You're not serious?"

"On this wonderful deserted beach. She didn't take any. She held me, helped me through it. I had the nightmare part I never told you about where I was in this jungle prison cage being poked and speared. But the rest was fantastic. Sometimes I can still pick up on it. I made it through, Jenny." He paused to look out into the night. "Mind if I light these candles. The overhead is so bright all you can see in the glass is ourselves." He lit four candles on the table and turned off the light. "No sex, but...but I can't describe it very well. So much more, so much better than any sex could be.

"Jenny, remember that time, we were married about two months, just had bought that new Alamo futon? It was so full, fluffy, so crisp and white. It was a week day, a Tuesday or Thursday when I was off and you didn't have class until ten. We were lying there about six with not even enough light to call it dawn yet, and I was on my back and you turned into me, put your arm across my chest. We didn't speak or do anything. Just lay there. Maybe an hour like that: silent and together on the verge of dozing, and it was like all of our words were being said in silence and the world was in perfect harmony."

"I finally stretched, lifted up and kissed you, said something like, 'God, what was that?' And you said you didn't know but it was unbelievably beautiful."

"That's a lot like what I felt with Erin."

"I never went to class," she recalled. "We walked in the park. Lay out there in the shade all day. Just goofed off."

"So close, like soul to soul. No games. Nothing to prove and knowing the 'all rightness' of that moment. I learned a lot from the acid about the moment, right now."

Jenny poured them more wine. "I guess I could never compete with that."

"There's no competition, Jenny. You and I, for that single magnificent day, had something like it. It's so hard to make into words. Like this aura, a Presence you step into or it covers and permeates you. I don't know which."

"I remember." Jenny got up and went to the bathroom.

When she came back, Ted saw that she'd been crying. He was clearing dishes and couldn't help himself from going up behind her and putting his hands on her shoulders as she opened the refrigerator to get out the pudding. "Jenny, what is it?"

She moved to the sink counter, leaving his hands hanging in space. "What is there to say, Ted? Sometimes I think I'll never know what I really want, so it's hopeless to think I can ever know another person."

Ted carried two spoons to the table and sat down. The candles had burned a quarter of the way down. Their flames were unmoving in the still air. "I've been feeling like that too, for a long time. You know that. And from this class too. I mean, all these elaborate and detailed rituals, the dos and don'ts, rights and wrongs that millions of people follow unquestioningly, just like here, like we do in the west."

"Why is it that I can love my family but can hardly talk to them? Today, when I saw my mom, all she could talk about was our divorce and how wrong it was, me moving in with Jerry.

Never a word about whether I'd learned anything, how I was
doing, or whether it was a terrible nightmare I was now
regretting. I always thought we were so close."

"But, Jenny, remember where she's coming from, what
her life has been? What she was taught to value. It's how I felt
coming home. I was ashamed, angry, but it was like your
friend's painting. They want you to put the past away in some
drawer. Forget it. And, Jenny, I could never make you
understand that. I couldn't put it away.

"If that was all life came down to in its truest moment,
why care, why get involved? How could there be any meaning
in my going into law if the ultimate litigation was killing each
other? Or into investments based on an economic system where
poverty is not only accepted but expected as the cost of doing
business? Where people our age get eaten up and, when we turn
fifty, spit out by the corporation. Power one day, nothing the
next. A lifetime of running scared." Ted was pacing up and
down the kitchen, and she reached out for his hand and gently
pulled him back to the chair. "That's what I thought the Age of
Hope was supposed to change. It was about dreams, getting
away from a running scared life and taking that Presence, that
aura we just talked about, and setting it down softly like a
blanket of light that transformed everything into the opposite of
what the world has become."

As he spoke, Jenny had lifted his hands into her own. "I
didn't know, Ted. When you returned, I saw you the way we'd
learned to see each other, like we'd been trained and educated.
Living by someone else's will: parents, teachers, brothers and
sisters, politicians, ministers. Somebody else's. But you
couldn't anymore. And I never saw that. I can see that with my
mom now too." She settled his hands on the table and let go. "I

better get back. He calls at nine every night. He'll wonder if I'm not there: the jealous type."

"Probably he worries, Jenny." She looked obliquely at him.

VI

Jenny held him around the waist, pressing her head into his back, her hair going wild behind them as they traversed the hills under a high bluish fog moving down and across the city. The lights were out in the house up the block where the old man lived.

Ted insisted on checking every room and closet, the doors. She went to the dark kitchen and poured a single glass of wine. He came out in a minute. She stood by the window where the North Star would eventually appear. "Can we sit down?"

"No, I don't want to stay. You understand. Especially after tonight."

"Yes. Will we talk again?"

"If you like."

"What about you, Ted.

"I'd like that."

"Do you really think talk can help someone become more than just another cardboard cutout?"

"Maybe, I don't know, Jenny. It's a start. Me. I know after the acid that I'm just a twenty-six year old kid who doesn't know very much. It can be the Age of Hope, Jenny. Or once was. Still is to me. I'm still trying for that, whatever it is. I'm not giving up"

"I doubt if love ever comes from talk."

"Old Socrates was living proof of that." They laughed and she hugged him.

"I want to toast." Jenny raised the glass and they held the stem, his fingers gently wrapped over hers. "Here's to...our Age of Hope? You drink first, Ted."

He drank. "And, maybe to authentic lives, Jenny."

She drank and put the glass on the table, turning to the window. There wasn't a sign of the moon. "Maybe, if we dare, Ted."

About the Author

I was born in a manger, actually a large and sturdy cardboard box filled with straw, in an alley next to the main L.A. railroad station. I never knew my parents because I heard it whispered that the birth was divine and my parents were forced to leave town under cover of darkness. I played with others like myself in and around the station and attended the school the railroad ran in exchange for carrying railroad luggage 10 hours a day for two bowls of rice and some greens. I was suddenly adopted by a world-famous writer whose "writer's block" I filled for 20 years, learning the craft that would pester me to this day. Eventually, I managed to find a wonderful woman and we started a family by the sea where we remain. If you need any further information, please use highway 101 phone box number 348 about 10 miles north of Goleta, CA.

Made in the USA
San Bernardino, CA
27 April 2018